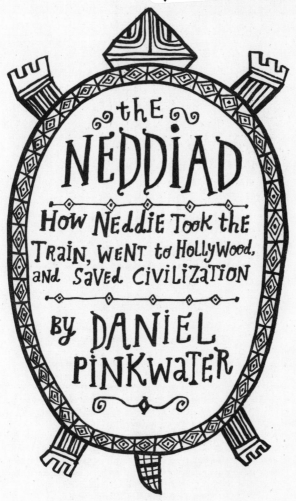

THE
NEDDIAD

HOW NEDDIE TOOK THE TRAIN, WENT TO HOLLYWOOD, AND SAVED CIVILIZATION

BY DANIEL PINKWATER

Illustrations by Calef Brown

sandpiper

Houghton Mifflin Harcourt
Boston New York

Library of Congress Cataloging-in-Publication Data

Pinkwater, Daniel Manus, 1941–
The Neddiad: how Neddie took the train, went to Hollywood,
and saved civilization / written by Daniel Pinkwater.
p. cm.
Summary: When shoelace heir Neddie Wentworthstein and his family take the
train from Chicago to Los Angeles in the 1940s, he winds up in possession
of a valuable Indian turtle artifact whose owner is supposed to be able to prevent
the impending destruction of the world, but he is not sure exactly how.
ISBN-13: 978-0-618-59444-3 (hardcover)
ISBN-10: 0-618-59444-2 (hardcover)
ISBN-13: 978-0-547-13367-6 (paperback)
[1. Turtles—Fiction. 2. Los Angeles (Calif.)—History—20th century—Fiction.
3. Humorous stories.] I. Title.
PZ7.P6335Ned 2007   [Fic]—dc22   2006033944

Manufactured in the United States of America
VB 10 9 8 7 6 5 4 3

Contents

CHAPTER 1

We Take the Train

I didn't always live here. And by "here" I do not mean the La Brea Tar Pits, where I am writing this down in a notebook—I mean Los Angeles. When I was a little kid I lived in Chicago.

On Wilshire Boulevard, in Los Angeles, there is a restaurant shaped like a hat. It is called the Brown Derby, and that's what it looks like—one of those derby hats, with the round top and the little brim all around. There is a sign outside that says EAT IN THE HAT. And people do. I knew about this because I saw pictures in *Look* magazine. The pictures showed the restaurant, the EAT IN THE HAT sign, and two movie stars—I think it was Bette Davis and Laird Cregar—inside the hat, eating cheeseburgers. They were eating cheeseburgers with knives and forks! This was interesting too. I had only found out about cheeseburgers a short time before—and had actually eaten only two of them. I did not know that some people eat them with knives and forks, but I thought of them as grown-up and sophisticated food even before learning that movie stars ate them.

Anyway, when I read about the Brown Derby and saw the pictures, it became one of my life's ambitions to eat there. I have to confess, I was not clear about exactly where Los Angeles, California, was—if it was not too far, maybe I could get my father to drive us over one day in the Buick.

So I mentioned it to my father, and I learned two things. I learned that Los Angeles, California, of which Hollywood is a part (the reason that movie stars eat in the Brown Derby), was way out West, and it took more than two days to get there by train.

The other thing I learned . . . Well, this is what my father said: "Neddie, my boy! It is also *my* lifelong ambition to eat in the restaurant shaped like a hat!"

And this is what he said next: "Not only will we eat in the hat, we will all go and live in Los Angeles, California! We can eat in the hat all the time, and pick lemons off the trees, and live in the sunshine."

A week later, we had packed up our clothes,

moving men had come and taken away the furniture, I had said goodbye to my friends forever, and my father, my mother, and my sister, Eloise, and I were on the Super Chief, which is a fancy deluxe train that goes from Chicago to Los Angeles.

You might think there was something weird about my family—my father, anyway—and there is. He is unpredictable and tends to do things that surprise people, until they get used to him. My mother seems normal at first, but she's married to him and always goes along with his ideas—like the parakeets, for instance.

I bought a parakeet for ninety-nine cents at the dime store. Little blue parakeet. I named him Henry. At the back of the dime store they have this pet department: goldfish, canaries, and parakeets. The usual price for parakeets is a dollar and a half, but they sell the shrimpy ones for ninety-nine cents. A dinky wire cage costs twenty-five cents, and the guy in the pet department threw in a box of birdseed for free. My father thought Henry was the greatest thing he'd ever seen, and a week later he came home with eleven more, a big cage with a parakeet playground, ladders and bells and perches and mirrors, a book on parakeet care, and bags and bags of stuff for them to eat. After a week of playing with the parakeets and reading up on them, he made it my job to take care of them: clean the cage, spray them for mites, smear Vaseline on their feet—also, I was supposed to train them to hop onto my finger, and teach them to talk. The talking never worked out—probably because we had so many of them. The book said that in order to teach a parakeet to talk, you needed to isolate it and repeat whatever word you wanted it to learn while it was going to sleep at night, and again the first thing in the morning. With a dozen parakeets, they just talked to one another, chirping and whistling and screaming.

I didn't mind being the family parakeet-keeper, but it was a lot of work. Also, I felt sorry for my parakeet, Henry, because all my father's birds were bigger, and they picked on him and made him miserable. My father liked to let them fly around the apartment, the whole flock of them, whirring through the air and pooping on things. When it was time to put them back in their cage, I had to catch them one by one, which wasn't easy.

What worried me was that he might bring home more parakeets—or something worse. Sometimes he would talk about monkeys.

"I am looking for a monkey," he would tell me. "I just missed getting one—no bigger than this," he told me, showing me with his fingers how little it was. "When I went back to the pet store, someone had bought it. But don't worry, Neddie. We will find a monkey."

I did worry. I worried a lot. I worried that he would find not one monkey but twelve monkeys. Those were going to be hard to catch—and they probably bit a lot harder than parakeets.

"Don't you think it would be nice to have a dog?" I asked my father. "Just a regular dog?"

"You should have seen this monkey," my father said. "He was just like a tiny person."

I think maybe there was already a plan to move to Los Angeles and everybody just forgot to tell me about it, or maybe not. My mother was used to my father, as I said, and when he announced we were moving across the country in a week, she just started getting things ready. Eloise seemed to be all right with the idea as far as I could tell. She is a lot older than I am, was in high school at the time, and didn't discuss things with me very much.

Or, maybe my father really had thought of it on the spur of the moment when I asked him about the eat-in-the-hat restaurant. My father is an eccentric. I didn't know that word at the time, but I knew he was one. He's not crazy or anything like that. He doesn't rave or flip his lips with a finger and go *bibble, bibble*. He just does things such as suddenly move his whole family to California, or travel in a deluxe double drawing room on the Super Chief with a bunch of parakeets.

The Second World War had ended a few years earlier, and my father came out of the war a rich man. He had gotten rich selling shoelaces to the army and the navy. Brown shoelaces to the army and black shoelaces to the navy. Before the war started he had gone to this auction. An auction is where they put things up for sale and people holler out how much they are willing to pay and the highest bid gets it.

He was at this auction, and one of the items was a large lot of shoelaces—it turned out to be a boxcar full of them. He won the whole thing for fifty-seven dollars. It turned out that along with the shoelaces came a shoelace-making machine. All this machine does is put the little metal or plastic tips on the ends of the shoelaces—the actual shoelace stuff comes in big rolls. You want fourteen-inch shoelaces, you put the little metal tip, which is called an aglet, every fourteen inches; you want a sixteen-inch shoelace, you put the aglet every sixteen inches. He got more machines and had a shoelace factory. After the war, my father invented plaid shoelaces, and shoelaces in colors like pink and bright blue. People bought millions of them.

And this is why my father was rich, and why we were on the deluxe Super Chief going to Los Angeles without a care in the world.

It was exciting to be on a train trip. My father had booked a double drawing room—that's two of the largest compartments, with the wall between them folded open to make something like a tiny apartment, with two tiny bathrooms, armchairs that turn into beds, and long benchlike sofas that fold into beds at night, also beds that fold down out of the wall, and you climb a little ladder to get in. The walls and ceiling were made of steel, painted pale green, and the floor was carpeted. There was a little white button on the wall, and when you pressed it you'd hear a bell go *ding* somewhere far away and a Pullman porter would come.

There are these guys, Pullman porters, black guys with deep voices, elegant manners, and starched white jackets. When you travel in a double drawing room, the porters give you extra-good service, because you are obviously somebody important or rich. Our porters were Mr. Frederick and Mr. Jefferson. They called my father Mr. Wentworthstein, which is our name, and brought us newspapers, playing cards, and ice-cold 7-Up, which I had never had before. My father said that 7-Up was the perfect beverage for train travel, and I agreed with him.

Looking out the window I saw other travelers hurrying to get on the Super Chief, redcaps—who are guys with red caps—rolling carts piled high with luggage, chefs in white coats and those tall chef's hats, loading boxes and boxes of things to cook into the dining car. There were conductors in blue suits with shiny brass buttons, the engineer in striped overalls, various railroad guys checking the wheels—everyone hustling and bustling—plus hot, steamy smells and powerful buzzing and hissing noises. The train itself was like a big living thing, like a dinosaur or a giant snake. You had to go up some steep steel steps to get into it. Once you were in it, it smelled . . . like a train—I didn't have anything to compare it to—it smelled of leather and clean carpeting, and hot motor oil, and rich people.

There was a lot of scurrying around and getting settled into the double drawing room. Mr. Frederick and Mr. Jefferson made sure all our suitcases were on board; the conductor, in his blue suit, came by and punched our tickets with a shiny silver ticket puncher. We looked out the window again. The rush of people on the platform was thinning out, getting slower. There were clunks and thumps as the steel stairs were folded up, and the doors banged shut. Some of the people outside the train were friends and relatives of people who were taking the trip. They waved and made faces at their friends who were on board. Guys in blue railroad suits wrote things down on clipboards and looked at pocket watches.

"All aboard!" somebody hollered. The people on the platform took a step back from the train. More bumps, thumps, and bangs. A guy in a railroad uniform, looking annoyed, walked fast alongside the train, up toward the engine. Then he walked back the other way. Everybody on the platform was standing still, facing the train.

Then we felt a bump, then a bump the other way. Nobody said anything. Another bump. The people on the platform were sliding to the left. Poles and columns and baggage carts too. We were moving! I could feel the wheels rumble under us. Slowly, slowly, the train was moving out of the station!

"Let's let the birds out of the boxes," my father said. "They need a little exercise."

My father was busy setting up his Zenith portable radio, a big thing, almost like a little suitcase, covered in black bumpy leather. It had the patented Wave Magnet, which was an oval plastic object the size of two dessert plates, with suction cups—this you'd stick to the window, and there was a flat ribbon-like cable that connected it to the radio. My father had bought it specially for the trip, and we were going to hear all the usual radio programs while we crossed the country in style.

My mother was leafing through a magazine, and Eloise was reading a book about art history. From Eloise's expression, and what I knew about her personal tastes, I was pretty sure she was pretending she was traveling with some other family—one with no parakeets or little brothers—or maybe alone.

As the train came out of the darkness of the station and into the semidarkness of the railyards on a gloomy winter afternoon, with the parakeets whirring and whizzing around the double drawing room and my family sipping 7-Up, I felt a kind of excitement I had never felt before. I knew I had begun my first big adventure.

Up to now, all my adventures had been either small or completely imaginary.

CHAPTER 2

The Childhood of Neddie Wentworthstein

You might think that a kid suddenly taken away from the only home he had ever lived in, his friends, his neighborhood, his school, would be a little sad, or worried, or have some kind of regret. I didn't.

I didn't at all. And this was not because I wasn't happy where I was. I was very happy. I would use these words to describe my early childhood at 551 East Roscoe Street in the city of Chicago: *interesting, fun, exciting, comfortable,* and *perfect.*

The reason I wasn't bothered at all about leaving our apartment, the backyards, the block, the neighborhood, and all the kids I knew was that I was a big fan of D'Artagnan. D'Artagnan is a character in a story called *The Three Musketeers*. We used to pronounce his name "Dar-tag-nan," but Ronnie Wolfspit explained to us that the right way to say it is "Dart-Onion," because it is a French name. Anyway, D'Artagnan is this guy who leaves home and has adventures. He goes to Paris and meets the three musketeers and becomes a great swordsman, and has a cape and a big hat with a big feather. We all wanted to be him.

I'd better explain about Ronnie Wolfspit and the other kids, and the games we played. First you have to picture what 551 East Roscoe Street was like, and where it was. Picture a street with all kinds of houses on it. Ours was made of brick, and had four apartments stacked one on top of another. There were stairs inside in the front, and stairs outside in the back, and wooden porches, painted gray, on each floor. On one side, there was another apartment house just like ours, and the two shared a backyard, where there were the usual clotheslines, and some parts paved and some parts dirt. There were the remains of a crummy vegetable garden that nobody took care of, and usually a few stalks of corn in the summer. This was an attempt at a Victory Garden, which people were supposed to grow to add to the food supply, because of the war. Of course, everybody where I lived was city people and had no idea how to take care of a vegetable garden, so it was a complete failure.

On the other side of 551 East Roscoe Street was a big white wooden house, like a farmhouse, with only one family in it, and a porch all around. Next to that was an apartment house eight stories high, with an elevator. In the other direction, next to the apartment house just like ours, was one with two apartments and a big front lawn. All kinds of houses on the one street.

There were also all kinds of kids. The backyards were connected—either there were no fences or there were gaps in the fences, so it made one big space. We kids owned the backyards. We had our own world in the backyards.

The adults were working all the time, so older kids were in charge of younger kids. My sister, Eloise, was supposed to watch me, which meant she sat on the back steps, reading or doing her homework and not watching me at all. I think the idea was that she was there in case somebody started to actually kill me.

The kids really in charge of the little kids were the slightly younger older kids, like Ronnie Wolfspit. Ronnie was in seventh grade, and he did not so much take care of us as supervise the games.

These are the names of some of the games we played: Bunker Hill, Gettysburg, San Juan Hill,

Verdun, Iwo Jima. Those are all battles. We were soldiers. Ronnie, or one of the other older kids, but usually Ronnie, would tell us which side we were on and what to do. Mostly what we did was run at each other with swords or shoot at each other with guns. We got most of the swords and guns by pulling boards out of an old fence. We all practiced dying, and everybody was good at it. The battle games were good—we all got to run around and yell, and we got dirty and everybody got to die repeatedly.

Another category of games had names like The Three Musketeers, 20,000 Leagues Under the Sea, The Hunchback of Notre Dame, Moby Dick, Mysterious Island, and From the Earth to the Moon. These are books. The older kids had read them, either in book form or in the Classics Comics version. These were better than the battle games because you got to be a character. One of the best parts was Captain Nemo, who was this weird crazy guy who had his own submarine. Ronnie Wolfspit did an excellent Quasimodo, the hunchback of Notre Dame. I can still see him, dragging Ruthie, the little girl who lived in the basement apartment, up the back steps, hollering, "Sanctuary, sanctuary!"

In addition to having us act out the books, the older brothers and sisters used to read to us little kids.

They didn't read little-kid books to us—they read what they wanted to read. Ronnie Wolfspit was a big Jules Verne fan, for example, and my sister, Eloise, seemed to like books about bloodthirsty pirates. Sometimes my mother would read to me about Peter Rabbit as a bedtime story, when earlier in the day Eloise had been reading to me, and some other kids, about William Teach, also known as Blackbeard the Pirate, boarding ships and hanging people and slicing them with a cutlass. It was all good.

We also played Tarzan, Flash Gordon, and Superman, and Captain Midnight, which were movies and radio programs. The thing about all these games was that they were all about adventure. They were all about people going off away from their familiar homes to do important stuff. And in the world outside the backyards, it was like that. People were going off to war, and moving to different parts of the country to do different jobs. And people were arriving from places far away. Some of the kids were refugees—that is, kids whose families had escaped from Europe. There was Jan the Dutch kid, who always wore this brown overcoat, and Helmut the German kid, who refused to play Nazis in the battle games, and Luigi, whose salami sandwiches smelled better than ours.

I expected, we all expected, to do exciting things,

and be a hero, like Dart-Onion, or Hopalong Cassidy, or the Count of Monte Cristo. This is why going away on a big adventure all the way across the country seemed normal to me. It is also why, when I was taken to the Louis B. Nettelhorst Elementary School to begin first grade, I said I wanted to major in literature.

CHAPTER 3

More About My Childhood

The reason I knew how Luigi DePalma's salami sandwiches smelled was that they were his lunch when we went to the Julian on Saturday mornings. The Julian was a movie house on Belmont Avenue. I had heard about it for years before I was old enough to go there.

"It's a movie house for kids," Ronnie Wolfspit, or some other older kid, would say. "They have all great movies, and it's all kids in the audience. And— get this—in the lobby, the lights are made out of real wagon wheels, off a covered wagon, with bulbs attached! And they give away free comic books!"

The deal was, if you'd leave, they gave you free comic books—not brand-new ones, old ones with the covers torn off. They were necessary because kids would watch the movies and stay and watch them again. We all had lunches with us, so there was no reason to leave. Sometimes a mother, or older sister, would come looking for a kid, and walk up and down the aisle, hollering for him. Naturally the kids in the audience would holler too. There was a fair amount of hollering at the Julian—also wrestling, and throwing things, and spitting down from the balcony.

This was a typical program at the Julian: A Hoot Gibson Western and another Western with Tom Mix, or Lash La Rue. A third feature, maybe Sabu in *The Elephant Boy*, or some other good picture. Five cartoons. Two serials, which are movies broken up into episodes—there is an episode each week. In the beginning, it says, "In our last episode," and they show a little of what happened, so you can catch up if you missed it. In the end, it always looks like Flash Gordon, or Superman, or whatever cowboy, is going to get burned to death, or crushed, or fall from a cliff—and that's where it ends. Until the next episode.

After seeing everything twice, we would leave with our free comic books, imitating Ming the Merciless, Emperor of the Universe, who was Flash Gordon's archenemy. Ming was really evil, and an archenemy is worse than a regular one.

CHAPTER 4

Dinner in the Diner

Bells! *Ding-ding-dong!* Someone was going along the corridor playing a little xylophone. That's how they tell you it's dinnertime on the train. Then there was a knock on the door of our double drawing room. It was Mr. Frederick.

"Dinner is served in the dining car, Mr. Wentworthstein," he said to my father. "Shall I reserve a table for you in, say, an hour?"

"I don't want a whole big meal," Eloise said. "I'm dieting. Can't I just stay here and read my book?"

"I can bring the young lady a light meal," Mr. Frederick said. "Some clear soup? A small salad? A chicken sandwich? Skim milk?"

"Oh, that sounds nice!" Eloise said.

Eloise was deep into her fantasy that she was not related to us and was traveling alone. While we were in the dining car, she would sit with the parakeets and pretend she was someone in a movie.

She was missing a lot. An hour later, just after the train had crossed the Mississippi River and passed from Illinois into Iowa, we arrived in the dining car, my mother and father and me. It was the fanciest restaurant I had ever seen! The guy who meets you and shows you to your table was wearing a tuxedo. The waiters, more elegant black guys, had the whitest, crispest uniforms and aprons. The tablecloths were crisp and white too. The silverware was heavy, and it gleamed. So did the plates and glasses. Everything rattled and tinkled as the train rumbled along, but in a sort of classy and elegant way.

Our waiter was Charles. He was smooth. He was sharp. Just watching him put a plate on the table, you knew that he knew everything about food and being a waiter. If you wanted more ice water, he would be pouring it into your glass at just the moment you first knew you wanted it—and the way he poured it was perfect. It was impossible to imagine he might spill water, no matter how much the train rocked—but if he had, I'm sure he would have done it in a way that made you happy you were there to see it.

The way you order your meal on the train is to mark what you want on a card, then give it to the waiter.

This is what we ordered: Native Mountain Trout Sauté with Bacon ($2.75)—that was my mother's. The Broiler Special: Cup of Soup, Broiled Sirloin Steak, French Fried Potatoes, Fresh Vegetable, Sliced Tomato Salad with French Dressing, Choice of Dessert, Hot Rolls, Coffee, Tea, or Milk ($4.75)—that was my father's. Fried Spring Chicken, Southern Style ($2.20)— that was mine. The trout and the chicken came with the little cups of soup, and the hot rolls, and all those things, only my mother had potatoes au gratin and I had mashed.

There were four chairs at each table, and just the three of us, so Charles put someone else at our table with us. This is how they do things on trains.

"May this gentleman join you?" Charles asked my father.

"Certainly," my father said, and to the gentleman, "Please sit down."

My father had traveled on trains a lot in the shoelace business, and he knew all about them. Some of the porters and waiters and conductors knew him and greeted him by name. He knew there was a barbershop on the Super Chief, and he planned to get a haircut during the trip, and said I could have one too. He liked to sit in the lounge car at the very end of the train and write postcards, and he knew there was a little door in the wall of the drawing room where you could put your shoes—and during the night, someone would open another little door on the other side and take your shoes away and shine them for you.

So my father half stood up and gestured at the empty chair with his hand. Charles pulled the chair out and the gentleman sat down.

"I am Colonel Ken Krenwinkle," the gentleman said. "I am pleased to make your acquaintance."

Colonel Ken Krenwinkle had long silver hair and a droopy silver mustache. For a necktie he wore a Wentworthstein extra-wide shoelace, Model #174, Royal Blue, tied in a bow. He ordered the Golden Omelette with Fruit Macédoine ($1.70), saltine crackers, and a cup of Postum coffee substitute.

"No bread before bed, that's my motto," Colonel Ken Krenwinkle said.

The colonel had twinkling blue eyes. He was on his way from Rochester, New York, where he owned the largest used-car lot in New York State, to the West, where he had spent his boyhood.

"I knew the West in the days when the great buffalo herds still roamed the plains," Colonel Ken Krenwinkle said. "I knew the great men, the cowboys and gunfighters, the lawmen, and the great Indians. I knew Bat Masterson, and Wyatt Earp, and Sitting Bull.

"You know, young man," he said to me, "the Super Chief follows a route that existed centuries before there were trains. We are riding in comfort along a trail first traveled by the red men, then the Spanish conquistadors and the fur trappers.

"My own father and mother came west along the Santa Fe Trail in a Conestoga wagon—a prairie schooner. Thousands of people, caravans of pack mules, stagecoaches, farmers looking for land and prospectors looking for gold—they all came this way.

"The Super Chief travels only twenty miles in the great state of Iowa, and the city of Fort Madison is its only stop. The actual fort was built in 1808 to protect the settlers from raids by the Indians. The fort was attacked many times during the War of 1812. Finally the American soldiers burned their own fort in 1813 to divert warring Indians. The settlers escaped through a tunnel and made their way by boat down the river."

Up to now, I had been enjoying looking out the train windows into the night. Once in a while we'd rumble through a town, or past a farmhouse with the lights on. I could get a glimpse into the windows sometimes, and see families sitting at the table, or see people going about their business in the streets of the towns. But listening to Colonel Ken Krenwinkle talk made me squint my eyes and peer into the darkness.

"Kansas City in a couple of hours," the colonel was saying. "The official starting point of the old Santa Fe Trail. Bat Masterson and Wild Bill Hickok came through here, as did my dear mammy and pappy. Once we pull out of Kansas City, we'll be in the real West."

Colonel Ken Krenwinkle talked on and on, and asked my father questions about his travels, and the shoelace business. Naturally, Colonel Ken Krenwinkle had eaten in the Brown Derby lots of times, and knew movie stars like Tom Mix and Tim McCoy. At the end of the meal, the colonel and my father ordered Havana cigars and went off to the lounge car to talk more. Before they left, the colonel put his hand on my shoulder and said, "It is impossible for a boy with his wits about him to travel the Santa Fe Trail without discovering something. You're a boy with his wits about him, and you'll probably find a treasure along the way. If you should meet a Navajo shaman named Melvin, you'll be in luck, so keep your eyes open."

CHAPTER 5

Along the Santa Fe Trail

I kept my eyes open much of the night. My fold-down bed was next to the window, and while the rest of the family, and the parakeets, were sleeping, I could peel back the thick cloth window shade and peer out the corner. I watched the shadows of trees flash past the train. I saw sleepy towns and crossroads. Sometimes we'd pull into a station, and I watched railroad guys and passengers. But mostly I was thinking about things Colonel Ken Krenwinkle had said. I was imagining, and could almost see, Indians in war paint, riding horses, and cowboys on a cattle drive, or some sheriff shooting it out with a bad man in the streets of Dodge City, where we were going to arrive at six A.M.

Clouds lit by the moon looked to me like covered wagons on the Santa Fe Trail.

When I finally got to sleep, I dreamed about a Navajo shaman—and I didn't know what that was—named Melvin who was going to somehow get me started on some fantastic adventure.

Colonel Ken Krenwinkle was sitting at the next table at breakfast. Kadota Figs with Cream ($0.40), Oatmeal ($0.45), and an Individual Pot of Postum ($0.25). Eloise was with us this time, nibbling toast and sipping tea.

"Here we are in La Junta, Colorado, spelled with a 'J,' pronounced with an 'H,'" Colonel Ken Krenwinkle said to us, turning in his chair and speaking over his shoulder. "It means 'junction' in Spanish, and that's what it is—where the Santa Fe Trail meets the Cimarron Cutoff, at Bent's Fort. The mountain route was longer, but slightly less dangerous—the Cimarron saved ten days, but there was less water along the way, and more danger of attack by hostiles. Still, three-quarters of the travelers, among them my own ancestors, took it.

"See, in the distance—that's Pike's Peak, a hundred miles away. At 14,110 feet, it's the easternmost of the big peaks in the Rockies. The motto of the people heading for the Colorado gold rush in 1859 was 'Pike's Peak or Bust.'

"It was here, in my youth, that I belonged to a sort of improvised police force known as the Committee of Vigilance, and we shot it out with the Butch Cavendish gang in front of Fergussen's Mining Supplies and Delicatessen. Most of the Cavendish gang got away, including, I am chagrined to say, my uncle Slade Krenwinkle, a very bad man."

I was so excited. Colorado! Gunfights! This was better than movies at the Julian. And the country out the window was looking like the West now too! There were weird rock formations, and colors you don't see in Chicago, and silvery plants that Colonel Ken Krenwinkle told me were sagebrush.

"You were in gunfights?" I asked Colonel Ken Krenwinkle.

"Only when absolutely necessary," the colonel said. "In fact, my Indian name, when I lived with the Osage, meant, 'Only shoots when absolutely necessary.' My uncle was the black sheep of the family, and a source of embarrassment to us all. Wild Bill Hickok finally dealt with him in Tombstone, just as Uncle Slade was drawing his Colt's Navy .45 revolver, with no good intention."

After breakfast, my father and Colonel Ken Krenwinkle went to the club car to play cards with the four Marsh Brothers, who happened to be on board. I was very excited at first, thinking the colonel had said "Marx Brothers," but these were the Marshes, not the Marxes. They were sort of substitute, imitation Marx Brothers—they did the same sort of things as the Marx Brothers did in movies, only not as well. Their names were Gaucho, Harpy, Chicklet, and Gumball. I was disappointed, but I went along to watch them play pinochle with my father and the colonel. They were funny, but not all that funny. I got bored after a while, and went off to look out the windows.

CHAPTER 6

On the Atchison, Topeka & Santa Fe

I had only been on the Super Chief for part of a day, a night, and a morning—but it was starting to feel like I had never been anywhere else. I knew all the porters and conductors, and waiters, and a lot of the passengers. The rumbling, rattling, and the rolling of the train had become like my breathing and my heartbeat.

Back at home, in Chicago, which seemed a long time ago, my job, if you want to put it that way, was going to school, playing with my friends, listening to *Superman* and *Captain Midnight* on the radio, reading books, seeing movies at the Julian, and sort of observing what went on in the neighborhood. On the

Super Chief, my job was watching out the windows. It was an interesting job. There were times when I got sleepy—it was the movement of the train, and the fact that we were a lot higher above sea level than I had ever been—but I fought to stay awake, because I didn't dare miss anything.

About the time we left La Junta, something happened to the land, the unexpected colors and the rock formations and all. The stuff I was looking at started to make sense in a weird way. This is hard to explain, but I thought the actual land we were traveling through was telling a story. Watching it all go past the windows of the train was like reading a book, one you don't understand but one good to read just the same. There was the history story, and the stories Colonel Ken Krenwinkle told—and those were good to think about—but what I'm talking about is something about the actual rocks that can't be translated into words. One of those scientists who studies rocks, and how the earth was formed, might be able to explain it—part of it, anyway. I hope it doesn't sound too crazy to say that some of those mountains, and mesas, and towers were like . . . alive. Like alive and like animals or people, with personalities, and memories, and . . . well, that is the best I can do. I just knew I didn't want to miss any of it.

There were cattle too, and herds of elk, and Indian guys taking care of sheep. And the train went through people's backyards, Indian people, with outdoor dome-shaped ovens for baking bread, making pots—I didn't know. Someone pointed out to me the ruts left by the old Conestoga wagons where the trail ran alongside the rail bed. I saw a big rattlesnake coiled on a rock, and a longhorn steer that had fallen down a ravine and broken its neck. And I saw cowboys! Real ones! Those guys had a way of sitting on a horse that made it look so easy, so comfortable!

And everything was sharper, brighter, clearer—I don't know if it was because the air was purer, or because we were high up, or why, but everything I saw was cranked up, realer than real. I loved my looking-out-the-window job.

There were more meals in the diner, and more stories from Colonel Ken Krenwinkle. I had begun to catch on that some of what he said was fact and some was not. But I didn't care—they were all good stories. And there was sitting around in the double drawing room, looking after the parakeets and listening to cowboy music on my father's Wave Magnet radio, from the radio station in Trinidad, Colorado.

CHAPTER 7

The Indian Building

It felt like much longer, like days, but we had only been on the train for twenty-four hours when we pulled into Albuquerque, New Mexico.

"We're here for about an hour," Mr. Frederick told us. "If the family would like to take a little walk, stretch your legs, possibly acquire some souvenirs, you have plenty of time to do so. Just come back when you hear the conductor shouting 'All aboard!'"

We hopped off the train. The first couple of steps on firm ground felt funny—but good, familiar. There were train guys scurrying, doing things, and bunches of passengers milling around. Some people who had been missing exercise were striding up and down the platform, pumping their legs and waving their arms. There were genuine Indian people selling stuff spread out on cloths on a lawn, and behind them was a neat-looking building—the Indian Building. We walked along a little path and went in.

There was all kinds of great stuff inside! The ceiling was high, and there was a tall fireplace with the remains of a fire in it. There was the smell of wood smoke and sweetgrass in the air. Fastened to the stone chimney above the smoldering fire was a chief's headdress made of eagle feathers. There were pots, and dolls, and cloth, and ornaments spread out on tables. At one end of the room there was a loom set up, and two women were weaving something.

My mother and father and Eloise took a fast look around, and then you could tell they were done. The Indian stuff didn't interest them.

"Let's look at the station now," my father said.

"I want to stay here," I said.

"Don't wander away, and be sure to listen for the conductor," my mother said.

"Yes, don't miss the train," Eloise said.

"The station is supposed to have very good architecture," my father said. "Sure you don't want to come see it?"

"I want to stay here," I said. "I'll be fine."

I didn't know exactly why I wanted to stay in the Indian Building. It was extremely quiet. When you've been on the train for a long time, you forget that it is constantly making noise. You sort of tune out the rattles and rumbles and thumps and vibrations. There weren't many people in the Indian Building, and no one was talking. The only sounds were the sounds of the loom, whisks and muffled thumps.

I couldn't quite work out what the Indian Building was supposed to be. It was a little like a store, but it wasn't clear to me if the things in it were for sale. It was a little like a museum, but it wasn't set up like a museum—nothing was behind glass, and you could pick up and handle things. It reminded me, in a way, of the reading room in the Belmont Avenue branch of the Chicago Public Library. Same kind of quiet. Only instead of books, there were things.

I got interested in a figure carved out of bone, or maybe it was an antler off an elk or some animal like that. It was a crazy little dancing guy playing a flute. He was dancing, really dancing—he wasn't moving, of course, but he almost looked as though he could. I picked him up and ran my fingers over the smooth bone. I put him down, faced him this way and that way. He looked good, and different, from every angle.

Whisk. Thump. Whisk. Thump. The ladies at the other end of the room were working the loom. The little flute-playing guy was dancing. I could almost hear the music, in between the *whisk—thump*. I could almost hear drumming, fast and light. I imagined the little guy moving to the music with quick little steps, playing his flute. *Whisk-thump-thump-thump, whisk.*

The pots were shaped to fit the hollow of somebody's hand; they had designs on them in fine black lines. *Whisk-thump-thump-thump. Whisk.* Wood smoke. Sweetgrass. When the little guy danced, there would be guys gathered around a big drum, tapping it light and quick, and singing, their breaths fitting in between the drum thumps.

Well, I was getting what the Indian Building was. It was all one thing: the fire, the headdress, the flute guy, the loom, the stuff on the tables. You could look at everything a piece at a time, think about it, pick what you liked, or you could just be there and take it all in at once—and if you did that, it sort of all came alive, and you knew something.

That is what I was thinking when this guy said something. It was an Indian guy, not tall, not short, not young, not old, not handsome, not ugly—just this guy standing there. What he said was "Exactly right, kid."

"What's exactly right?" I asked him.

"You are. The way you're doing it. Exactly right."

"Feels right," I said. "How does it work?"

"Who knows?" he said. "But I'll tell you this—hundreds of people come in and out of here, and not many catch on. Here. Take this."

He took something out of his pocket and put it in my hand. It was a little turtle carved out of stone.

"What's this?"

"Little turtle carved out of stone. Take care of it at all times."

"Will it bring me good luck or something?" I asked.

"Possibly. I don't know. Just hang on to it."

"Is your name Melvin?" I asked.

"Yes."

"Are you a shaman?"

"In my spare time."

"It's a neat turtle," I said. "Thanks."

"Don't let anybody get it away from you," Melvin said. Then he said, "Train is leaving."

"All aboard!" the conductor was shouting.

I ran for the train.

CHAPTER 8

Mile 1,332 to Mile 1,691

Chicago is mile 0, Albuquerque is mile 1,332, and Flagstaff is mile 1,691. There are stops at Gallup and Winslow in between, and the train travels at an average speed of approximately seventy-two miles per hour.

In the station at Albuquerque, my father had bought two engineer's hats, made out of that soft stripey denim, one for him and one for me—they had the Super Chief insignia printed on the front. He also got us two red bandannas like the engineers wear around their necks.

My mother had gotten a whole stack of new magazines, and Eloise had bought a book about the route we were traveling on the Santa Fe Railroad. It was a pretty interesting book—I had a chance to have a look in it because Eloise had not finished the book she was already reading, about the Erie Canal in New York State.

Those are the things my family got in Albuquerque—and I had my turtle, which I did not show them.

It was typical of Eloise that she would want to read a book about the things that were rolling past the windows but hardly spent any time looking at them. In fact, none of my family was glued to the windows like I was. My father loved the train itself—which I did too. He was having fun ordering different things in the dining car, and talking with Colonel Ken Krenwinkle and the other passengers, and playing cards with the Marsh Brothers, and having his hair cut and his shoes polished.

My mother was the same wherever she was—except at home she liked to do household projects and was always taking down the curtains and washing them, and putting the curtains up, and shampooing the carpet, and polishing the walls. She'd get Eloise to help her. When she wasn't doing things like that, she would cook, and bake banana cake, and when she wasn't doing that she liked to take the bus downtown and buy things at Marshall Field's department store. In between, she would sit happily, flipping through magazines, looking for ideas about things she could cook, and things she could clean, and things she might like to buy.

It's not that they wouldn't have been interested in the turtle, and how I happened to have it—it was just that they would have thought it was in the same category as the things they had brought on board, and I knew it was something different. Something sort of secret.

CHAPTER 9

Left Behind

To this day, I don't know how I got confused in Flagstaff, Arizona. For some reason or other, I thought the train was going to make a long stop, the way it had in Albuquerque. I had been standing at the end of the corridor after supper, talking to Mr. Washington, when we pulled into the station. He opened the door and folded down the steps to the platform and went off to help some passengers with their luggage, and I just stepped down, meaning to stretch my legs.

I took a little walk along the platform. A street ran alongside the tracks, looking like a street in an old-fashioned western town. Another street led away up a hill, and maybe a block along, I could see a lot of lights, and people milling around, and horses—with cowboys on them! I could hear hoots, and *yippees* and *yahoos,* and guns being shot off! I looked both ways and ran across the street. It was chilly, but I had my sweater on, and my engineer's hat and neckerchief.

It just took a few seconds to go up the hill to what I supposed was the main street. There was some kind of cowboy parade going on! People lined the sidewalks, all the stores were lit up, and there was music playing. And the cowboys were all dressed up—so were the horses, with fancy saddles and bridles with lots of silver decorations. There were cowgirls too, looking pretty, on fancy horses. There were Indians in really nifty costumes with big war bonnets. People on the sidewalks were shouting and cheering, and the riders waved to the crowd and made their horses wheel and rear up on their hind legs. The cowboys also whooped, and once in a while one of them would shoot off his six-gun.

It was just great. I sort of squeezed between the adults and struggled right up to the curb with a bunch of other kids. Some of the horses were just fantastic—golden palominos, and paints, and spotted Appaloosas.

I loved it. And the town was great too—I liked the way everything looked. I wished I could stay longer, but I thought I'd better hurry back before the train left.

Of course, the train was long gone when I got back to the station. What's more, I hadn't been missed. I had free run of the train and went everywhere, so it would be quite a while before it dawned on any of my family that I hadn't been seen for some time. Then it would take time for them to decide that maybe they should go looking for me, and more time for them to realize that I was nowhere to be found. Add to this, as I found out later, it so happened that one of the parakeets had gone missing at the same time I did, and my mother, father, and sister were searching all over the double drawing room and out in the corridor for a good half-hour. It was Henry, my personal parakeet. They finally found him on top of the light fixture in one of the tiny bathrooms in our compartment.

In fact, they never did realize I was missing. They found out I was still in Flagstaff when Mr. MacDougal radioed a message to the conductor that he had me, and I was safe.

CHAPTER 10

The Tin Hat

By the time I got back to the station, the train was gone, whoever had gotten off the train was gone, the taxicabs were gone, and the baggage handlers and the railroad guys were gone. The waiting room was empty, except for one guy in a blue railroad suit with brass buttons. He was sweeping the floor.

"Hello, hogger," the guy in the blue suit said to me.

"Hogger?"

"Yes. Aren't you a hogger, a hoghead, a driver . . . an engineer?"

"Oh, because of the hat! No, I am not an engineer."

"I thought you looked a little young to be a hoghead, but then you might have been a young-looking midget. So, what do you do on the railroad?"

"I don't do anything," I said. "I was a passenger on the Super Chief."

"You're a peep? And you missed your varnish? The Super Chief is highballing and you're stuck out on track seven."

I didn't get a word of it. Mr. MacDougal explained that *peep* is short for *people,* meaning a passenger, a *varnish* is a passenger train, *highballing* means going down the track at maximum speed, and *stuck out on track seven* means you're screwed. Mr. MacDougal told me he was the tin hat, or station master.

"I'll radio a message to the pin puller—that's the conductor—and let him know where you landed. Come on into the office."

Mr. MacDougal talked into a thing that looked like a telephone. "This is Flag. Put the skipper on," he said. "I've got a pint-size peep on the siding. Missed his snoozer. Let me know what you want done with him.

"Have a seat, young man. The brains—that's the conductor—will tell your folks you're alive and kicking and radio back to me. Have you put on the nose-bag? The lizard scorcher at the Chuckwagon Café across the street could send over a sandwich."

I told Mr. MacDougal that I'd had my dinner.

"Well, just sit there and let off steam," Mr. MacDougal said. "We should get a message back pretty quick."

And pretty quick there was a loud buzz, and Mr. MacDougal picked up the receiver. Whoever was on the other end did most of the talking. Mr. MacDougal said "uh-huh" a lot, and wrote things down in a little notebook. Then he said, "Tell Mr. Wentworthstein that we'll make sure his boy gets there" and put the receiver down.

Then he picked up the regular telephone and dialed a number. "Charley, this is MacDougal down at the station. We have a stranded passenger, a young fellow. Can you fix him up with a room for the night?" Then Mr. MacDougal listened for a while, and looked at me. "I'll ask him. Neddie, are you a stable and steady young man?"

I told him I was.

"He says he is. Neddie, your nerves are good? You're not afraid of spooks and goblins, are you?"

I told him I was certainly not.

"He seems a manly little chap to me," Mr. MacDougal said. "I'll send him over. Railroad will pay, and collect from his dad. So long, Charley."

Mr. MacDougal fished a little book out of a desk drawer and filled out a form. Then he tore the form out of the book and handed it to me. "Sign this. It's a receipt for fifty dollars, for your expenses along the way, which the railroad is advancing to you, and your father will pay us back." He unlocked a drawer and counted out some bills. I signed the receipt.

"Now, here is the schedule," Mr. MacDougal said. "I am supposed to get you onto a train to Los Angeles—which will not be easy, since everything is booked up solid. When you get to Los Angeles, either your father will pick you up at the station or someone will put you in a cab to the Hermione Hotel, which is where your family will be staying. I've written down the name. Your folks will be there from tomorrow morning on. Tonight, you will stay up the street at the Monte Vista Hotel, which is jam-packed because of the cowboy jamboree in town, and has only one room available—and it's haunted. Do you have any objection to sharing with a ghost?"

"Uh . . . is it a nice ghost?"

"Very nice ghost from what I hear. I don't think it's the kind that keeps you up all night."

"In that case, it suits me fine," I said.

"Good lad. You can sign for your meals at the hotel. Come down here in the morning to see if I was able to get you on a train."

I thanked Mr. MacDougal and made my way up the hill to the Monte Vista Hotel.

CHAPTER 11

In the Old Hotel

You couldn't miss the Monte Vista Hotel. It was the tallest building in town, and had a big electric sign on the roof, in capital letters. I went in. The place was full of cowboys. A lot of them were in the bar, and a lot of them were standing around in the lobby, hitching up their belts and spitting into spittoons. I walked up to the desk. A guy with slicked-down red hair—I guessed it must be Charley—said, "You the kid? Here's your key. Room 107—it's up those stairs."

I looked around the lobby, and listened to the sound of spit hitting the spittoons. The cowboys were interesting to look at, and they were good spitters. There was a kid my age in the lobby. He was a hand-some kid, wearing a cowboy hat. He was leaning against the wall and spitting. He wasn't bad at it either. I went over and leaned next to him, and took aim at a spittoon.

"Not bad," the kid said.

"I practice a lot," I said.

"That's a neat hat," he said.

"It's a hoghead hat," I said.

"Mine's a Stetson," the kid said. "You want to trade?"

"For keeps?"

"Let's see how we look," the kid said. We swapped hats.

"How do I look?" the kid said.

"You look like a hogger," I said. "Try the bandanna."

"You look like a cowboy," the kid said. "You want to make the trade?"

"My father gave me the hat," I said.

"So? My father gave me that one. Your father a railroad man?"

"Shoelace man," I said. "Your father a cowboy?"

"Nah, movie star," the kid said. "I'm Seamus Finn."

"I'm Neddie Wentworthstein."

"My father is Aaron Finn. You know who he is?"

"Not sure."

"Did you see *The Three Musketeers*?"

"Wait! Is he the guy who played Dart-Onion?"

"That's him. He was Dart-Onion, and he was Count Luigi in *The Swordmaster*."

"He's good! Is he like that in real life?"

"Nah, he's an actor. He's in the bar, studying the cowboys so he can be one. Are you here with your father?"

"I'm on my own. I understand the room where I'm staying has a ghost."

"No fooling?"

"So I'm told."

"A real ghost? How do you know?"

"Come with me," I said to Seamus Finn. I walked him over to the desk. "Charley," I said. "Does room 107 have a ghost in it?"

"Yes, but it's not a real bad one," Charley said.

"It's really a real ghost?" Seamus Finn asked Charley.

"It's a ghost," Charley said. "You know, it appears, it vanishes. Would you say that was real, or not real?"

"When my father comes out of the bar, tell him I went with Neddie," Seamus said. "My father is the guy with the biggest cowboy hat."

"I know. Dart-Onion," Charley said.

CHAPTER 12

In the Ghost Room

I went with Seamus Finn to room 107.

"It's a little crummy," Seamus said.

"Do you smell that funny smell?" I asked. "Do you think that's a ghost smell?"

"I think it's a crummy-room smell," Seamus Finn said.

It may have been a little crummy. The furniture was sort of scuffed, and the rug was worn, and there was that crummy smell—but it was my own personal hotel room, and I was pleased with it.

"Take a seat," I said to Seamus Finn. He sat in the beat-up chair. "May I offer you a glass of water?"

"So, how come you're traveling on your own?" Seamus Finn asked.

I told him all about missing the train, and Mr. MacDougal, and how he was going to try to get me on a train to Los Angeles, only it was going to be difficult.

"There are lots of soldiers, and cowboys and families on vacation," I said. "I'm kind of hoping he winds up putting me in the crew car—or maybe I could ride in the engine."

"That would be neat," Seamus Finn said. "But I just got another idea. My father and I are going to drive back to Los Angeles pretty soon. I could ask him if you could come along with us."

"That would be great!" I said. "Nearly as good as riding with the engineer. I mean, driving with Dart-Onion and all."

"It's not all that interesting," Seamus Finn said. "I mean, he doesn't have a sword or anything. But we're going to the Grand Canyon tomorrow. I'll ask him. I'm sure he'll say yes."

"Ask him if I can come too," someone else said.

We both jumped straight up in the air. There was someone else in the room! We had forgotten all about the ghost for a minute.

"I'm serious. I take up hardly any room. Ask your father." The person doing the talking was a bellboy. I had only seen bellboys in movies and cartoons, but I knew what they looked like. This was a kid, maybe a little older than Seamus and me—he had a short red jacket with brass buttons and shoulder straps, one of those round bellboy hats, and a pair of white gloves under one shoulder strap.

"How'd you get in here?" I asked the bellboy.

"I just came in. My name is Billy. So, how about it? Will you ask your father if I can come along?"

I was noticing something about Billy, and Seamus Finn was noticing it too. He was just a little bit transparent. Seamus said, "Billy, is it my imagination, or can I sort of see through you?"

"No, it's not your imagination," Billy said. "I'm a ghost, as if you didn't know. I'm the Phantom Bellboy, and thanks for not screaming or acting like an idiot."

"So . . . you're . . . uh . . . dead?" I asked Billy.

"Well, I'm a ghost. You figure it out."

There was a long silence. Seamus sat in the chair, I sat on the bed, and Billy the Phantom Bellboy stood there, being slightly transparent. It was a weird feeling, being in a room with a ghost.

Seamus Finn was less uncomfortable than I was—probably came from growing up around movie stars and all that. "So, what, do you, uh, just haunt?"

"Pretty much," Billy the Phantom Bellboy said. "There doesn't seem to be much else to do. The truth is, it's fairly boring. That's why I'd like to come with you to Los Angeles."

"I'd have to ask my father," Seamus Finn said.

"I'm no trouble," Billy said. "I don't eat, don't take any space, and I'm very polite. At least take me with you to see the Grand Canyon."

Billy the Phantom Bellboy told us that what he did, day in and day out, was knock on the door of room 107 and then disappear. Sometimes he would let the guests get a glimpse of him, and sometimes he just wouldn't be there when they opened the door. "And that's it. That's the whole routine. Tell me, how long would it take you to get bored with a job like that?"

"Are you able to leave the hotel? I thought ghosts had to more or less stay in one place."

"I go across the street to the bakery sometimes," Billy said. "They have good sweet rolls."

"I thought you didn't eat," I said.

"I like to sniff them," Billy said. "Take me with you. I've had it with this town."

There was a knock on the door. I opened it and there was Aaron Finn, looking like a movie.

"Father, this is Neddie Wentworthstein," Seamus Finn said. "He got left behind by the Super Chief and is trying to get to Los Angeles. I told him maybe he could come along with us."

"I don't see why not," Aaron Finn said. "But I'd need to speak to someone in charge of you."

"You can tell Mr. MacDougal at the railroad station," I said. "And my parents will be at the Hermione Hotel in Los Angeles tomorrow morning."

"We'll give them a call," Aaron Finn said. "And, if it's all right with them, you're welcome to come with us. And who is this?"

"This is Billy," Seamus Finn told his father. "He's the Phantom Bellboy. He's a ghost."

"Really?" Aaron Finn said, peering at Billy. "A ghost, eh? I do see he is rather transparent. This is excellent. I've never met a ghost. I might have a part as a ghost sometime. So you're a ghost, are you?"

"Dead as a doornail," Billy said.

"Billy wants to come with us too," Seamus Finn said.

"Absolutely! Welcome, Billy. I seem to remember there was a script with a very good part for a ghost. I suppose you know all about being one, do you, Billy?"

"I know what there is to know," Billy said. "I'm the real thing. Do you think I could find something to do in Hollywood, Mr. Finn?"

"Oh, yes—technical advisor sort of thing, I'm sure. You come with us, young man—or is it old man?"

"I'm fifty-seven, if you count from when I was born," Billy said.

"Imagine that," Aaron Finn said. "Well, let's discuss this at breakfast."

"I'm not supposed to go into the dining room," Billy said. "It upsets some people."

"I can't imagine why," Aaron Finn said. "Well, in the morning then. We'll make arrangements for Neddie here, and then it's off to the Grand Canyon. Very pleased to have met you both."

Aaron Finn and my new friend Seamus Finn went off to their deluxe room, Billy the Phantom Bellboy went to do some haunting, and I turned in, in my very own hotel room.

CHAPTER 13

On the Road

It had all gone perfectly. After a very good breakfast (I had oatmeal with raisins, toast, orange juice, milk, and scrambled eggs, $2.50—I signed for it, and Aaron Finn showed me how to add 25 cents for the tip), Aaron Finn put in a call to my father at the Hermione Hotel.

"Mr. Wentworthstein, this is Aaron Finn, the actor," Aaron Finn, the actor, said. "My young son has made the acquaintance of your fine boy, Neddie, and we would be most happy to deliver him to you in Los Angeles in two or three days. In the meantime, we are going to explore the Grand Canyon, the local Indian ruins, and natural wonders."

My father was delighted. He asked to speak to

me, and I told him that the railroad had advanced me fifty dollars, and that Mr. MacDougal said it would be hard to get me on a train. My father was perfectly happy with the arrangement. "I don't suppose any harm can come to you if you're traveling with Dart-Onion," he said.

We stopped off at the railroad station, where Aaron Finn explained everything to Mr. MacDougal, and then we were off in Aaron Finn's huge Packard convertible, which was about as big as a double drawing room.

Billy the Phantom Bellboy was pretty near invisible outdoors in daylight. You could just make him out if he stood in the shadows and you squinted—and even then, you'd have to know you were looking for him. He was very quiet as we drove out toward the Grand Canyon. I think he was happy.

Billy sat up front with Aaron Finn. Aaron Finn was wearing his French foreign legion hat, the kind with the little brim in the front and the handkerchief attached in back—he had saved it from the foreign legion movie he'd been in, *March or Don't*. Seamus Finn and I sprawled out in the back seat, and talked, and watched the landscape go by.

It was a whole lot different from looking out the windows of the Super Chief. For one thing, windows on trains don't open, so there's always a piece of glass between you and whatever you're looking at. You can't feel the air, and you can't smell it. Also, the train is sort of high up—you're above the land. In the car, you're lower down: you're in it. It's not like a picture sliding past. You can taste the dust, especially in an open car.

There was plenty of dust. Also, beautiful mountains in the distance, and all the sorts of things I had seen from the train, except we could have stopped and gotten out anytime we wanted. It was only eighty-one miles to the Grand Canyon, and we only stopped once, so Billy the Phantom Bellboy could go behind a rock. None of us felt like asking him why.

During the ride, I told Seamus about life in the neighborhood, and the Nettelhorst School, and the usual things I had done. I was surprised that he thought it all sounded really nice, and he wished he could live in a place like that. Seamus Finn went to a boarding school, which meant he slept there, and ate there, and saw his parents only once in a while. His school was called Brown-Sparrow, and it was a military school. His mother lived in New York, and he'd visit her a couple of times a year, and a few times she would visit him. His father was always off acting in movies, so it was the same with him.

Actually, it sounded great to me. I had really loved staying in my very own hotel room the night before, and I loved traveling without my family. Brown-Sparrow sounded more interesting than the Louis B. Nettelhorst Elementary School. The kids wore uniforms, fancy ones, and marched around like soldiers. He told me the place looked more like a college, with nice big buildings with ivy growing on them, and everything was fancy and first-class. You didn't bring your lunch in a greasy paper bag or get horrible slop in a hot, steamy cafeteria—they had a big dining hall, and ate off china plates. They had a band that played every day while they marched to lunch.

Seamus explained that military schools had been popular about twenty years before, and there were still quite a few around. People in the movie business made lots of money, and liked to show off, so they sent their kids to these places. A couple of retired movie actors named Brown and Sparrow had started his. All the male teachers were dressed up as captains and majors, and everybody had to salute each other and say "sir." I told Seamus that it sounded like fun, and I wished I could go there.

"Well, BS—that's what we call it—is not that bad," he said. "But sometimes you get tired of it and wish you could just live with one or more parents. If I went to the Nettelhorst School, I would bring salami sandwiches every day, like that Luigi kid you told me about."

One useful thing Seamus Finn told me was that there was a movie house on Hollywood Boulevard called the Hitching Post that sounded exactly like the Julian, only maybe better.

"Do you go there on Saturday mornings?" I asked him.

"Always," he said.

"Neat. I'll be seeing you there," I said.

CHAPTER 14

Grand Canyon

It had been less than two days since I had left Chicago. In that time, I had ridden on a deluxe streamlined train, talked with an old gunfighter and a lot of other people, seen all kinds of landscape I'd never seen before, been given a stone turtle by an Indian shaman, seen cowboys, and been left behind in Flagstaff, where I had my own hotel room, made a friend, and met a ghost and a movie star.

Standing on the south rim of the Grand Canyon topped all those experiences put together. I couldn't believe it! I mean, I couldn't believe it. It was so big, and so complicated, and so beautiful, and so unexpected that I had a hard time accepting that it was real. Seamus Finn said it hit him the same way. He said he kept thinking it was some fantastic big painting, or a movie set. There was a little building put up by the park service, with a model of the Grand Canyon made out of plaster and painted to look real. It had little cards on it, telling you what was Bright Angel Trail, and what was Point Sublime, and what was Mooney Falls. In some strange way, looking at the model was more comfortable than looking at the actual thing. After looking at the model for a while, we went outside and found we were able to deal with the real canyon a little better.

Besides being un-understandably big, and having all the amazing colors, and having such clear air that everything stood out sharper than real, the thing the canyon made you want to do was go down and be inside it. We wanted to just step over the edge of the rim and start climbing down, which people do—there are trails and you can hike down, or ride down on mules. Billy the Phantom Bellboy, being a ghost, didn't need a trail and was already a couple hundred feet down the side, and having a wonderful time.

Aaron Finn had a better idea. He was arranging for us to take an airplane ride. We whistled and hollered for Billy to come back, which made us look crazy to the tourists, because they couldn't see him in the bright light. Then we piled into the Packard and headed for the place where the airplane would take off.

I had never been up in an airplane. I was pretty sure this was turning out to be the best day of my life. Then I saw the airplane and I was completely sure. It was a Ford Tri-Motor, the smartest airplane ever made.

Let me tell about the Ford Tri-Motor, or "Tin Goose." They started making them around 1929, and only ever built about two hundred of them. As the name suggests, it has three motors, one on the nose and two mounted below the wings. They are all 450-horsepower Pratt and Whitney Wasp R-985 nine-cylinder radial engines. The fuel tanks hold 355 gallons, and the plane uses about 80 gallons per hour. It is a high-wing monoplane, with fixed landing gear, just under fifty feet long, with a wingspan of seventy-seven feet, ten inches, and can carry fifteen passengers and two crew. I knew all this because it was printed on the box my model airplane kit of the Tri-Motor came in. And, I might add, it is the greatest airplane ever built, and smelly and noisy with lots of vibrations—which just makes it better somehow.

We all started smiling when we saw the aircraft. Just looking at it was enough to make us happy—

knowing we were going to take a ride in it, and through the Grand Canyon to boot, was almost too much to deal with. Billy the Phantom Bellboy said this was the best thing that had ever happened to him in his whole death.

CHAPTER 15

My Yiddishe Shaman

It was going to be a few minutes until the plane took off. They were waiting to see if any more people besides us turned up. So we stood around the little airport, looking at the airplane and at the nifty souvenir tickets we'd been given. There was a guy, a mechanic or something, Indian guy, not tall, not short, not young, not old, not handsome, not ugly—just this guy. I looked at him. He looked at me.

"Melvin?" I asked.

"Sheldon," he said.

"Oh. You look like a guy named Melvin."

"I know. And you're the kid with the turtle."

"You know about the turtle?"

"Take good care of it. It's important. I see you're taking Billy for an outing."

"Wait! You know Billy?" I asked.

"Sure, Melvin knows me, and I know Melvin," Billy the Phantom Bellboy said.

"It's Sheldon," I said.

"Did you tell him your name was Sheldon?" Billy asked.

"Yes." Sheldon smirked. "Just fooling with his mind."

"So you're really Melvin?" I asked.

"No, I'm really Irving," Sheldon/Melvin said.

"Does he know about the turtle?" Billy asked.

"He just knows to hang on to it, and it's important," Sheldon/Melvin/Irving said.

"You know about the turtle?" I asked Billy.

"It's important. Hang on to it," Billy said.

"Wait. What . . . ?"

"Time to board the plane," Sheldon/Melvin/Irving said. "Have a great flight."

CHAPTER 16

Down in the Sky

I love flying! I love flying! I love flying! As soon as I get old enough, I am going to take flying lessons, and if I get rich and have my own plane, it's going to be a Ford Tri-Motor! Never mind that it's so noisy, you have to yell at the top of your lungs. Never mind that it buzzes and vibrates. Never mind that it smells of burned oil and exhaust fumes enough to make a ghost throw up, which is something I'd rather not witness again. It's just a great aircraft, and I wouldn't have any other kind.

The pilot was Jack Lacheln. He was handsomer than Aaron Finn, and had a leather jacket, a white scarf, and sunglasses. When he saw him, Aaron Finn whipped out a little notebook and sketched a picture of him—obviously so he could be made up to look like him if he ever played a pilot in a movie.

We were the only passengers on the plane, except for an evil-looking little guy. This guy wore a hat with the brim turned down all around, had a greasy mustache, wore a black suit, and smelled like lilacs. He introduced himself to us. His name was Sandor Eucalyptus. Before we took off, Sandor Eucalyptus asked Jack Lacheln if he could have a parachute.

"There are parachutes under the seats," the pilot told him. "But you have no need to worry. The aircraft is completely safe. We've been flying it for twenty years, and it works perfectly." Good old Ford Tri-Motor.

"Just the same, I would prefer to wear my parachute," Sandor Eucalyptus said.

"Really, it isn't necessary," Jack the pilot said. "If we were to crash, which is just incredibly unlikely, you'd be safer going down with the plane than trying to use a parachute if you don't know how."

"Just the same," Sandor Eucalyptus said. "In my home country, the Duchy of Botstein, it is required by law that all passengers wear their parachutes, and I am simply used to it—if you please."

"Well, if you insist," Jack said.

"It's Botstinian custom," Sandor Eucalyptus said,

strapping on his parachute. Aaron Finn was sketching Sandor Eucalyptus.

"I must ask you for that drawing, señor," Sandor Eucalyptus said, reeking of lilacs.

"It's just a hobby of mine," Aaron Finn said.

"Please indulge me," Sandor Eucalyptus said. "I have many little prejudices. I dislike pictures of me to be made."

Aaron Finn tore the page out of his notebook and handed it to the evil-looking, parachuted little man.

"What a jerk," Seamus Finn whispered to me.

"Really," I whispered back.

We forgot all about Sandor Eucalyptus as the Tri-Motor took off, and soon we couldn't smell him for the fumes from the engines.

"The Grand Canyon is two hundred and seventy-seven miles long," Jack Lacheln shouted at the top of his lungs. "It's eighteen miles wide at its widest point, and six thousand feet—more than a mile—deep at its deepest. It's been cut by the Colorado River for the past six million years, and you can see the strata of rock that show two billion years of our earth's geologic history." The plane was rising into the air, and I had never felt so good in my life.

"There is evidence of human life in the canyon dating back three to four thousand years," Jack shouted. "Around a thousand years ago, the Anasazi people farmed in the canyon, and developed a rich culture, and the present-day Hopi people consider the canyon their ancestral home. And in Havasu Canyon, which is one of the many side spurs, the Havasupai people are still farming today.

"The Grand Canyon was set aside as a forest preserve by President Benjamin Harrison in 1893, and was proclaimed a national monument by President Teddy Roosevelt in 1908."

Jack kept talking, but I wasn't listening. What I was seeing was too incredible to pay attention to anything else.

Now that I come to it, I can't say what it was like. I barely had time for it to sink in that we were up in the air, above everything—and then we dipped down, into the canyon, and we were below everything and above everything at the same time. We were flying inside the earth! I was hardly breathing. I don't think I blinked.

"Jack!" I shouted at the top of my lungs. "What's that down there?"

"Turtle Rock?" Jack shouted back. "That's a natural rock formation—or maybe a paleolithic carving—experts disagree—looks like a red-eared turtle. Considered very important by the Hopi people. Has some kind of ritual meaning—something to do with preserving the world, or protecting the world, or something."

It was exactly like my turtle, the one the turtle-shaman, Melvin, or whatever his name was, had given me!

"Oh, you noticed that it's just like your turtle," Billy the Phantom Bellboy said. "Interesting coincidence, isn't it?"

Jack took the plane up again—now we were high over the canyon, making a slow, sweeping turn.

"What turtle is that?" Aaron Finn asked.

"I have a stone turtle," I said. "A shaman gave it to me."

"May I see it?" Aaron Finn asked. I handed him the turtle. Aaron Finn held it in his palm. "This is fine," he said. "It's evidently very old. Wonderful thing."

"Let me see it, Father," Seamus Finn said.

Aaron Finn handed the turtle to his son. Seamus looked at it closely. "Really. Wonderful," he said.

"And now you will give the turtle to me, young man," Sandor Eucalyptus said. We saw that he was holding a gun, a small silver one. "Just give it to me, and please, no one move." Sandor Eucalyptus was standing up in the aisle between the rows of seats. "Quickly! Hand it over!"

Seamus Finn plunked the turtle into Sandor Eucalyptus's outstretched hand. He gripped it in his fist, then shoved it deep into his pocket. Then, keeping the gun trained on us, he moved backwards toward the door of the airplane. Still facing us, he reached for the handle of the door. He turned the handle. He opened the door.

"And now, *signori . . . auf Wiedersehen!*" Sandor Eucalyptus said, and hurled himself out of the airplane.

We saw him falling. His hat blew off and floated after him. Then his parachute opened, and we watched him drift down, out of sight into the depths of the Grand Canyon.

"Well, that was a first," Jack said. "The fellow is obviously as crazy as a bat. Going to be a lot of trouble finding him—assuming he survives the parachute drop, or the canyon itself, a tenderfoot like that. We'll have to go back to base now and make a report to the police."

It was all sort of shocking. I couldn't say anything at first. Then I said, "He took the turtle."

"Yes, it was too bad about that," Seamus Finn said. "I'm sorry, Neddie, sorry I handed it over to him—but he was holding a gun on me. You see how it was."

"Yes, of course," I said.

"I couldn't do anything else," Seamus said. "I just plunked it in his palm—like this—here, Neddie, hold your hand out."

I didn't know why Seamus was going on about it. We had all seen what happened. But he took my wrist and made me hold my hand out, palm up—and then he plunked something into it. It was the turtle!

"What? What? How'd you . . . ? You! What?" I said.

"Here, I'll show you. Give it back to me," Seamus said.

Aaron Finn was grinning broadly. I gave Seamus the turtle and he plunked it into my palm again—only this time when I looked it wasn't the turtle—it was a jellybean!

"Mmmm, it's a black one," Seamus Finn said. "Eat it up, Neddie. I hope Mr. Sandor Eucalyptus enjoys his jellybean after his parachute ride." Seamus Finn handed me my turtle.

"Seamus has special permission to leave the school on Tuesday nights to attend the magicians' club at Joe Berg's Studio of Magic," Aaron Finn said. "Fine work, son. Worthy of a Finn."

I thought it was fine work too.

CHAPTER 17

Box of Weasels

"So, it's your belief that the gunman was of unsound mind?" the sheriff's deputy asked Jack Lacheln.

"It's my belief he was as crazy as a barn owl," Jack Lacheln said. "Crazy as a loon. Crazy as a bedbug. A bun short of a dozen. A nutcase. Crazy as a box of weasels."

"And what makes you say that?" the deputy asked.

"Well, he smelled like the perfume counter at Woolworth's, he insisted on wearing his parachute, then he got excited and made this gentleman give him a little drawing he'd made, and after that he pulled a gun on everybody, made this lad give him a little stone turtle, and jumped out of the airplane. I'm no psychiatrist, but I don't call that normal behavior."

The deputy wrote in his notebook: *Crazy as a box of frogs.*

"Box of weasels," Jack Lacheln corrected him.

"Hardly a chance in the world we'll find him," the deputy said. "Probably broke his neck, or else he's wandering around the canyon, raving mad, eating small animals. Would you say he's dangerous?"

"As a box of rattlesnakes," Jack Lacheln said.

"Or a box of Gila monsters?" the deputy asked.

"Yes, I'd say so."

"I'll put that down, *box of Gila monsters,*" the deputy said. "Does anyone have anything to add?"

"Yes," Seamus Finn said. "I . . . " But Aaron Finn gave him a stern look and shook his head slowly. Seamus stopped speaking.

"My boy here wanted to mention that the gentleman claimed to come from foreign parts, and spoke several languages," Aaron Finn said. "If you have no further need for us, we'd like to continue on our way."

"No, I don't suppose you'll be needed," the deputy said. "I don't suppose we'll ever find the fellow either. Probably a mountain lion will eat him. But we'll go down on mule-back and have a look. I'm sorry about this unpleasant interruption, and I hope you'll enjoy the rest of your trip."

In the Packard, Seamus Finn asked his father, "Why didn't you want me to tell about the neat way I substituted a jellybean for the turtle? I did it really well. You know, if you plunk a small object into someone's palm, they'll tend to close their fingers around it. I learned that at the magicians' club—it's called the French substitution."

"It was neat," I said. "And you knew he would shove the thing in his pocket. In his excitement, he never noticed that the jellybean was smaller than the turtle."

"It was very neat," Aaron Finn said. "But obviously Jack Lacheln, busy piloting the noisy aircraft, missed the bit about you substituting the jellybean, and thus said nothing about it to the deputy. It might be best to let people think that Sandor Eucalyptus got away with the turtle. Just in case anyone else is thinking about coming after it."

"You think he meant to get it on purpose?" I asked.

"You don't think he was merely as crazy as a box of frogs?"

"Box of weasels," Aaron Finn said. "And it pays

to play it safe. I had a part in a spy picture once, and the situation was . . . well, actually, it was nothing like this, but all the same, I think it is best not to let too much be known. Now, who's for lunch? Anyone hungry?"

"I could sniff a bowl of chili," Billy the Phantom Bellboy said.

"Capital idea," Aaron Finn said. "Let's be on the lookout for an authentic taqueria."

CHAPTER 18

Scorched Lizard

"**T**his looks like the place," Aaron Finn said as he pulled the Packard up in front of a broken-down-looking building, with a sign on the roof that said EAT. Painted over the door was LAGARTO CHAMUSCADO—COLD BEER.

"It looks a little crummy, Father," Seamus Finn said.

"Oh, that's how you can tell it's the real thing," Aaron Finn said. "We're going to have a royal feast here, mark my words."

It was hard to tell if the place was even open for business or just an abandoned old shack. There were no cars parked outside, the windows were thick with dust, and it was just sitting all by itself way out in the desert. We piled out of the Packard and followed Aaron Finn inside.

Once we got in, it was a little better. There were rough wooden tables, and benches, a fire crackling in the fireplace, and an extremely nice smell. No people, though.

An enormous guy, well over six feet tall, with a big belly, wearing one of those tall chef's hats and a white apron, came through a little door at the back of the room. His face was all red and shiny, and he had a black mustache that curled up at the ends.

"Gentlemen!" the guy in the chef's hat said. "Welcome to Lagarto Chamuscado! Please be seated, and I will wait on you."

We took seats on two benches. "May we see a menu?" Aaron Finn asked.

"The menu is in my *toque blanche*," the enormous guy said, pointing to his chef's hat. "I am Antonio Frantoio Del'Fagiolo, graduate of the Culinary Academy of Belgium, diplomate of the Institute of Cookery of Rome, and I also attended the Cooks and Bakers School of the United States Army. Today we have Navajo fry bread, Hopi corn stew, cheese and green chile soup, blue corn dumplings, of course, green chile paste, yucca pie, wolfberry jam, and Hopi tea. Also Coca-Cola and Dr Pepper. What is your pleasure?"

"How about a little bit of everything?" Aaron Finn asked.

"I was hoping you would say that," Antonio Frantoio Del'Fagiolo said. "I will now busy myself in the kitchen, and in a short while, you will begin a meal which will surpass your wildest dreams of happiness. While you await your spectacular repast, would you care to whet your appetites by snacking on these tortilla chips and salsa? We have hot, dangerously hot, and foolhardy." He placed a basket of oily-looking chips and three cracked bowls of green stuff on the table, then disappeared through the little door.

"I wonder which salsa is which," I said.

"I'll tell you," Billy the Phantom Bellboy said. He sniffed each of the three bowls. "This one is okay. This one will test your nerves. And this one will cause you to see visions. Be careful with this stuff—this is how I died."

Aaron Finn then explained to us that the thing about eating hot foods is not to let them know you're afraid of them. Still, I noticed that after sampling salsa number one and salsa number two, he never touched number three. None of us did.

It's amazing that I was able to taste anything after the salsa, but I was. Antonio Frantoio Del'Fagiolo brought plate after plate of wonderful things I had never seen before, but every one of them tasted like an old friend.

"Did I or did I not tell you this was the right place?" Aaron Finn said. We all said things like "ummph," and "mmmm," and "yum," except Billy, who said *snfff*.

While we were eating, Antonio Frantoio Del'Fagiolo pulled up a bench and sat watching us. Nobody was talking much—we were too involved with the food. All anybody said was "Please pass those blue things," and "Try some of this," and "May I have more of that?" and "Yum!"

After a while, it sort of came to an end, and we looked around at each other. Everybody looked happy. Antonio Frantoio Del'Fagiolo poured cups of tea. "So, best meal you ever had in your lives, wasn't it?" he said. "And this one has been eating on the Super Chief, which is famous for good cooking."

"How did you know I was on the Super Chief?" I asked Antonio Frantoio Del'Fagiolo.

"You're the kid with the turtle, aren't you?" he asked me.

"And how did you know that?" I asked, excited.

"There's a medicine man, comes in here all the time. He loves my blue corn dumplings, and who wouldn't?"

"Melvin?" I asked.

"That's the one. He told me you'd be coming in."

"And how did he know that?" I asked, more excited.

"Like I said, medicine man. He knows all sorts of things. He told me to give you a message when you came in."

"He did?"

"He did. Now, what was it? Oh, darn, I can't remember. He said, this kid who has the turtle—that's you—would be coming in with some other people, and a ghost—that's how I was sure it was you—and I was supposed to tell you . . . It's right on the tip of my tongue."

"So you have no trouble seeing the ghost?" Seamus Finn asked.

"Billy? I see him fine. I eat my own cooking, you know. If you eat that foolhardy-grade salsa, you'll see all kinds of things. Oh! I remember the message! It's 'Get out of this country. You're in danger.'"

"In danger? What kind of danger?"

"He didn't say. Just 'Get out, you're in danger'—that's the whole message."

"Why didn't he tell me himself? I saw him only a couple of hours ago."

"No idea. So, what did you think of the food?"

CHAPTER 19

Get Your Kicks on Route 66

"Ah, Route 66, the Mother Road, the Will Rogers Highway." Aaron Finn was behind the wheel of the Packard. "Now we'll see what this baby will do. I'll bet we can make Los Angeles in six hours flat. Now everyone put on your goggles."

Instead of putting the top up, Aaron Finn had goggles for everyone in the car, although Billy the Phantom Bellboy couldn't wear, and didn't need, his.

"This is a historic highway, boys. You'll see many interesting sights flash past in a blur. Someone make a note of the time and mileage—we're out to break the record to L.A.!"

There were some questions I wanted to ask Billy the Phantom Bellboy.

"What do you know about my turtle?" I asked him.

"That it's important, and you should hang on to it?" Billy said.

"In many Indian creation myths, the world is said to have been created when certain animals, such as the muskrat, brought mud from the bottom of the Great Water and piled it on the back of Big Turtle—then trees grew, and so forth, and the world is carried on the back of Big Turtle. In fact, to this day, most indigenous peoples refer to North America, or the world in general, as Turtle Island. And the turtle looms large in Chinese and other Asian mythology, also African, and South American—pretty much the same sorts of stories, and the same sort of significance. There are even Eskimo turtle stories, though there's not a turtle to be seen in the Arctic. If that's any help," Aaron Finn said.

"How do you know all this stuff, Father?" Seamus Finn asked.

"I have an encyclopedia in my trailer at the studio," Aaron Finn said. "There's a lot of waiting around while they set up the cameras and lights."

"What do you know about Melvin, the shaman?" I asked Billy.

"He's unusual," Billy the Phantom Bellboy said. "The average Navajo will go out of his way to have nothing to do with a ghost. It's *chindee*—that's like taboo, or forbidden—but Melvin is open-minded, probably because he's a medicine man, though some suspect he's not really Navajo. In any event, he's a nice guy."

"Do you know why he gave me the turtle, and why that guy in the airplane tried to take it, and why Melvin sent a message that I would be in danger if I didn't get out of there?"

"Nope. My guess is, he gave it to you because he saw that you were the right one to give it to. But I don't really know anything about that other stuff."

"Well, thanks anyway," I said.

"And if I knew any more, I wouldn't tell you," Billy said. "Ghosts can keep a secret."

Billy the Phantom Bellboy and Aaron Finn got into a conversation about the history of the movie business, and old-time movie stars who had stayed in the Monte Vista Hotel and been haunted by Billy. This topic interested both of them, and it was clear they would be at it for hours. It was also clear that Billy was not going to give me any information, if he had any, about the turtle, or Melvin the shaman.

Seamus Finn and I adjusted our goggles and watched the scenery go by. It was nice, riding and not talking. The conversation about William S. Hart and Charlie Chaplin and Theda Bara droned on in the front seat, and soon blended with the rush of air and the hum of the motor.

The big Packard was flying along the road, leaving a cloud of dust behind it. Route 66 was interesting. We went through long stretches of desert, and every so often we'd come upon something completely unexpected. These are some of the things we passed: ghost towns, signs pointing to old mines, rusted-out diners, trading posts, fancy hotels, drive-in movies where you watch from your car, a meteor crater, lots and lots of roadside zoos with signs for miles before, saying SEE THE FIVE-LEGGED LIZARD, a barbershop with a car on the roof, and motels shaped like teepees, a whale, an airplane, a windmill, and a huge duck. When it got dark there were animated neon signs in a lot of colors.

We only stopped for gas, plus once, when we were across the state line in San Bernardino, California, at McDonald's fifteen-cent hamburger stand, where you Buy 'Em by the Bag. "This is a good idea," Seamus Finn said. "They should open more of these."

I'd like to take another ride on Route 66, and go a lot slower.

CHAPTER 20

Another Old Hotel

We pulled up outside the Hermione Hotel. "Look at that!" Aaron Finn said. "Six hours and twenty-seven minutes! And remember, we stopped for gas, and hamburgers, and there was that delay in Barstow when the burros were standing around in the road. I think we made excellent time!"

The Hermione Hotel was a big white building, covered with stucco and eight stories tall. Stucco is this stuff that looks like oatmeal. Aaron Finn explained that the Hermione was the fancy place to live in the days of silent movies. Rudolph Valentino and a lot of other big movie stars used to live there. It wasn't a regular hotel where you check in for a night or two, or for a week's vacation. Instead of just rooms, it was all apartments, with kitchens—and people lived there for weeks, or months, or all the time. My family was cooking supper when we arrived.

"*Whoop!*" my mother screamed when she saw Billy the Phantom Bellboy. "It's another one! Roger! Call the management! Tell them they have to move us again!"

"The first apartment they put us in had ghosts," my sister, Eloise, explained. "So they moved us to this one."

"This is Billy," I said. "He's with us."

"He may not stay here!" my mother said. "Mr. Ghost . . . Billy, you may not haunt this apartment!"

"We're just delivering Neddie," Aaron Finn said. "Billy will be leaving with us."

"This place is just full of ghosts," Billy said. "I can tell. Just chock full. It's the ghostiest place I ever saw, living or dead."

Now my sister screamed. "Aaron Finn! I mean, Mr. Finn! Oh! It's such an honor to meet you! I . . . " and then my sister fainted. She actually fainted. She sank to the carpet. I looked at Seamus Finn.

"Happens all the time," he said.

"I never knew Eloise was such a movie fan," I said. Eloise was sort of writhing around on the carpet, moaning softly.

"We're just about to sit down to dinner," my father said, stepping over Eloise and shaking hands with Aaron Finn. "Won't you join us?"

"Well, the truth is, we filled up on fifteen-cent hamburgers a while ago," Aaron Finn said. "But we'll keep you company, if we may."

"I'd like to have a sniff of what you're cooking," Billy the Phantom Bellboy said. "Is that meatloaf?" It was the right thing to say. My mother was proud of her meatloaf.

"I'm sorry if I was rude just now," she said to Billy. "The ghost in the first apartment they gave us moaned and wailed so."

"I hate that," Billy the Phantom Bellboy said. "Your mashed potatoes smell delicious."

"I have a bottle of fig wine I bought at the Hollywood Ranch Market," my father said. "And cold root beer for the young men. Are you sure you wouldn't like some meatloaf?"

While my family ate, I looked around at the apartment. Everything in it came from around 1927. It was all normal-looking, but a little bit different. The stove and refrigerator weren't like any I had seen, and the knives and forks and dishes were just a little different too. The furniture and lamps had a funny, unfamiliar look.

Aaron and Seamus Finn and Billy the Phantom Bellboy told my family about our adventures, except for Sandor Eucalyptus, and jumping out of airplanes, and Melvin the shaman. They stuck to seeing the Grand Canyon and driving on Route 66. Of course, they couldn't leave out ghosts in the Monte Vista Hotel, because Billy was sitting right there. Billy told some stories about haunting people and said he was happy to be visiting Los Angeles.

Aaron Finn asked if the parakeets were adjusting to their new home nicely. Eloise, who had gotten over her faint, said she thought they seemed to be. My mother told about our trip on the Super Chief, and wondered if Aaron Finn had ever met the Marsh Brothers.

"Mr. Finn, I wonder if you could advise us about schools for the children," my father said.

"Well, I understand the city high schools are excellent, and I am certain Miss Eloise will do very well," Aaron Finn said. Eloise blushed over her mashed potatoes.

"But for Neddie here, I suggest you look into the Brown-Sparrow Military Academy, which my own son, Seamus, attends."

"Seamus is a very polite boy," my mother said.

"They teach us to be polite at Brown-Sparrow,

Ma'am," Seamus said. "And also to take care of our clothes, and be neat and tidy."

"Seamus plays the bassoon in the junior band," Aaron Finn said. "And last year he received a medal for English grammar."

"I imagine the uniforms are very smart," my mother said.

"They were created by one of the finest costume designers in Hollywood," Aaron Finn said.

"Oh, Roger!" my mother said. "Wouldn't it be nice if Neddie was very polite, and had a smart uniform? Let's send him to Brown-Sparrow!" Seamus Finn and I looked at each other.

"I think we should certainly look into it," my father said.

CHAPTER 21

Getting Settled

Aaron Finn, Seamus, and Billy the Phantom Bellboy said goodbye. Seamus told me he hoped I would be coming to Brown-Sparrow. I was sorry to see my friends leave. We'd been through a lot together.

I was shown my bedroom, which was actually a sort of sun porch, with big windows all around, stucco walls, a cement floor painted dark green, a bed, a wicker chair, and a wicker desk. Wicker is . . . I don't know what wicker is—it looks like long noodles woven together. It's the sort of furniture they used to have on porches, especially back in the 1920s. It was an okay room, I thought.

Then the floor began to shake, and the glasses and cups rattled in the kitchen cupboard.

"It's an earthquake," Eloise said. "We've had two before this. We're used to them already."

"Tomorrow we'll go around looking things over and continuing to get settled in," my father said. "And I think we should have lunch . . . guess where?"

"Eat in the hat?" I asked.

"Eat in the hat," my father said.

CHAPTER 22

Looking Around

"I demand you enroll me in an accredited high school this very morning," Eloise said.

"Don't you want to go with us and look at Los Angeles?" my father said. "What's the difference if you start school a few days or a week or two later? Neddie is going to have a good time driving around in the keen yellow Cadillac I rented, eating in hats and seeing the sights. Don't you want to come too?"

"I do not want to get behind in my work," Eloise said. "Besides, it is the law that you have to send your children to school. I do not want to go driving around with you people like the grapes of wrath. I want you to take me to Hollywood High School and sign me up at once."

When Eloise makes up her mind, her mind is made up. There's little to be gained by trying to argue with her. So we finished our Grape-Nuts of wrath, and our first stop of the day was at Hollywood High, where Eloise was duly enrolled, and we left her there. Then we rolled off in the yellow Cadillac, which was not as grand as Aaron Finn's Packard, but it came close. This was my first look at Los Angeles, and there was plenty to look at.

It's not possible to sum up a big city—especially a city that's a couple hundred years old and made up of all kinds of things, natural and man-made, and contains all kinds of people—in a few words. But if I had to sum up my first impression of Los Angeles in a few words, I would say it's a perfect combination of glamorous and crummy.

First of all, it's got palm trees, which are strange-looking, and the more you look at them, the more you realize how strange-looking they are. Then there are the buildings—you see an ordinary house, then right next to it a very elaborate house, maybe with towers and turrets and balconies—right next to that is a place that sells tires, or shoes, or lawn furniture, completely square and normal-looking, but with a huge sign that rotates. Then you see nice mountains in the distance, or a beautiful garden—then a house that is shaped like a milk bottle—probably it was a store that sold dairy products when it was built, but now someone lives in it. A little way down the street will be an apartment house that looks like an Arabian palace. Then a sweet little cottage. Then a house shaped like a mushroom, with polka dots. And then a real, genuine, hundreds-of-thousands-of-years-old water hole, with a lifelike, but fake, statue of a real, but extinct, animal in the act of drowning in the middle of it. (That's the La Brea Tar Pits—I'll tell more about it later.) You get the idea—the rules of reality are always getting bent, or at least dented.

My father had a theory about the houses. He said it was all because of stucco. This is how they build a house in Los Angeles. We saw some houses being built this way—first they build a frame out of wood, in the usual way. Then they staple heavy black roofing paper onto the frame. Next, they staple chicken wire on top of the roofing paper—that's to hold the stucco. Stucco is a kind of goo, sort of like cement. They glop it on the outside, and they glop it on the inside. It hardens up, and—*bing!*—the house is done!

Now here's my father's theory. When you're building things that way, it won't be long before someone says, "Hey! I can make this thing any shape I want! Look, I can make the whole house look like a giant pickle!"

Which is why you see things like the hot dog stand that looks like a hot dog on a bun, or a restaurant shaped like a hat, which was our destination as it got to be noon.

CHAPTER 23

Exploring

The thing about eating in the hat, about eating in a restaurant shaped like a hat, is . . . it's a restaurant. Shaped like a hat, of course. But once you get over that, it's just a restaurant. My cheeseburger was very good, and my mother and father had them too, and liked them—and some of the people eating there were probably movie stars, though we didn't recognize any of them. I have to say, it didn't measure up to the Lagarto Chamuscado, and I felt a little let down. Not so my father. He just loved it. He was happy as a clam. He was joyous. He was smiling from ear to ear the whole time. He was over the moon. He was tickled pink. He was eating in the hat.

After lunch we did more touring. We parked the

car and took a walk. We saw Hollywood and Vine, which is famous. Why it is famous I cannot say. It is an intersection. Hollywood Boulevard meets Vine Street. There's a traffic light. There's a drugstore. There are people walking around. Some of them are tourists—they are the ones taking pictures of Hollywood and Vine.

We walked along Hollywood Boulevard, which was mildly interesting. There were stores, movie theaters, hotels, restaurants. Then we came to Grauman's Chinese Theatre. That was interesting. It was this big building looking like a Chinese palace or temple. It was very fancy. There was a sort of courtyard in front, where movie stars had pressed their hands, or feet, or hands and feet, in wet cement, and scratched their names. We walked around looking for the hand- and footprints of movie stars we liked. And we bought some popcorn at the little store to one side of the courtyard. The thing I liked about Grauman's Chinese Theatre was that with all the fancy you could buy a ticket at regular prices and go in and see a movie.

We crossed Hollywood Boulevard and walked back along the other side. We found the Hitching Post, the movie theater Seamus Finn had told me about. It looked good—it had wagon wheels outside. I thought maybe I would go over to Brown-Sparrow Military

Academy before long and see Seamus. Maybe I could meet him at the Hitching Post on Saturday morning.

Then we came upon the greatest store in the world. We went in and looked around. This store was brilliant. It was a big store, and in the back it had magic tricks—not just little ones, but big professional ones involving mummy cases, and Chinese cabinets, and all kinds of shiny equipment with gold paint and lots of colors. This reminded me of Seamus Finn again, who was a member of a magicians' club. I thought he must know about this store—probably bought tricks here. I knew a couple of simple card tricks, but I was no magician. Looking at all the neat equipment, I thought maybe I might learn a little more.

The middle part of the store was all model airplane kits! Here was something I knew about. I am pretty good at building models. They had some pretty fancy big models hanging on strings from the ceiling. And besides model airplanes, they had model ships and trains. There was a model of a clipper ship, the *Flying Cloud,* all built and finished, with complicated rigging made out of thread. And they sold the kit to build it. $9.95. It looked like it would take a year. Pretty nice ship, though.

In the front part of the store, in glass cases, they sold a variety of things anybody would want—

harmonicas, switchblade knives in all sizes, and big chrome-plated rings with Indian heads and skulls with rubies for eyes, all with lots of sharp corners, so if anyone got slugged by someone wearing one, it would hurt. As I said, the greatest store in the world.

Oh, they also sold jokes. My father loves jokes. He bought a flower you wear in your buttonhole, with a thin tube that connects to a rubber bulb full of water you keep in your pocket. You invite someone to smell your flower, and when he bends close to smell it, you squeeze the bulb and the flower squirts him. A good idea, but the flower was completely fake-looking, a red rose made of plastic. Anybody would see what was coming. I pretended I was a regular citizen and sniffed the flower, and let my father squirt me. He thought it was great. I was pretty sure I was the only one he would catch with that thing. He asked me if I saw anything I wanted. I told him I needed to come back and think about that. There were too many choices—and I needed to decide if I was going to be a magician, the builder of the biggest ship model ever, or a knife-carrying, harmonica-playing practical joker.

CHAPTER 24

Real Exploring

We wandered around some more and then took to the Cadillac again, drove up and down streets aimlessly, and then came upon the La Brea Tar Pits. I knew right away that it was the greatest thing in Los Angeles.

My parents didn't get it. They didn't see what I saw. This is what they saw: some ponds—little ponds, puddles, practically—with wire fences around them, three or four not-real-good statues of big weird-looking extinct animals, grass, some little signs telling what happened here 400,000 years ago, a cement building that looked like a garage, no people. If you looked at the surface of the ponds, you'd see bubbles coming up slowly, and if you walked on the grass, you might get tar on your shoes where the stuff was bubbling up. My mother got tar on her shoes and wanted to leave. My father said the statue of the drowning mammoth was okay, but he wouldn't mind leaving.

"Please, I want to stay here. I want to read the signs," I said.

"We'll go across the street and explore that big drugstore," my father said. "Don't fall in a tar pit."

It isn't tar. Everyone calls it tar, but it's really natural asphalt. The Indians used it to waterproof their canoes, and the Spanish settlers used it to seal their roofs. "La Brea" in Spanish means "the tar," so "The La Brea Tar Pits" means "the the tar tar pits."

What happened was, volcanic pressure forced petroleum up through cracks in the earth, and sand—the petroleum sort of rotted, and that's how it turned into black, sticky, gooey asphalt. These water holes formed, with water on top and asphalt on the bottom. In the winter, the asphalt was hard and everything was normal, but in the summer it warmed up and got soft and gooey.

Animals came and drank from the water holes. Now, picture this—a mastodon comes to drink. There's a bunch of wolves lurking in the underbrush. They come after the mastodon. Ordinarily, he'd try to break for open country, but there are wolves coming from all directions, so he runs out into the middle of the water hole. The wolves pile in after him. He's fighting and struggling, and the wolves are splashing around, trying to get hold of him. And then they realize they're all stuck in the goo, and sinking. They die. The asphalt slowly dissolves all their soft parts and preserves their bones, which float around, slowly, for 100,000 years. Some of them bubble up to the top, and around the year 1915 scientists discover them and start dragging them out. They get thousands and thousands of skeletons of extinct animals.

No dinosaurs, because all this started in the Pleistocene epoch, after the dinosaurs were gone. But plenty of other stuff.

The animal they found most of was the dire wolf, which was as big as the biggest modern wolf, and stronger, with serious teeth. The paleontologists pulled thousands of dire wolves out of the tar pits, which suggests to me that either there were lots and lots of them or they weren't too bright.

American lions, larger than the modern African kind, may have been smarter—not so many of them turned up as fossils. But the saber-tooth cat, or saber-toothed tiger, was another animal that couldn't remember not to jump into the water holes. Second greatest number of these found. Extinct, of course.

Other animals they found included mammoths, giant sloths, giant bears, camels (not very many—must have been smart), ancient bison, a kind of primitive horse, birds, reptiles, and turtles, it said on the sign.

It was very exciting to think that these water holes were just the same when ice age animals lived and died in the very place where I stood. Under my feet there were mammoths and mastodons, bears bigger than a grizzly, huge sloths, lions and wolves. It was as though they had just now been alive. The bubbles that rose from the tar might contain the last breath of some creature not seen on earth for 100,000 years. There had been humans here too. One of the signs told about La Brea Woman, the only human found in the tar pits. She lived 9,000 years ago, and is the oldest female human ever found. She was one of the ancestors of the Indian people who lived here later. La Brea Woman didn't fall into the tar pits by accident. She was murdered. Someone had knocked her on the head.

I felt in my pocket for my stone turtle. It felt warm. I was getting a feeling something like the way I felt that time in the Indian Building, only this feeling was wilder, and a little scary.

CHAPTER 25

Letters

"Look, we got you a book about the La Brea Tar Pits at the drugstore," my father said.

Great! Just what I wanted. I knew I was going to come back to this place lots of times. I wanted to know all about it. I didn't pay much attention to where we drove next. I was in the back seat of the Cadillac, reading about the Pleistocene. My mother annoyed me by insisting that the fossils in the tar pits were there as a result of the flood in the Bible. My father said that there was a joke going around during the ice age that Los Angeles was the tar pit of the nation.

"Well, here we are," my father said. "The Pacific Ocean."

The Pacific Ocean!?! I had forgotten all about the Pacific Ocean! Los Angeles has an ocean!

"It looks like Lake Michigan," my mother said.

The Pacific Ocean! I was looking at the Pacific Ocean!

"No, this is salty; Lake Michigan is fresh water," my father said.

"And this is bigger, right?" my mother said.

The Pacific Ocean! It's an ocean. It goes all the way to Asia. It's got Hawaii in it. It's got whales in it.

"Sure," my father said. "An ocean is bigger than a lake."

"Well, it's very nice," my mother said. "We'll have to come back sometime and spend the day." Sometimes I can understand why Eloise likes to pretend she's not related to them.

When we got to the Hermione Hotel, Eloise was there, back from Hollywood High School. "Look, Neddie, you got two letters," she said.

One was from Seamus Finn. It was on Brown-Sparrow Military Academy stationery. He said his father was in Canada, shooting a movie about Mounties, and Billy the Phantom Bellboy was with him. When his father got back we were all going to have lunch with him at the movie studio. Meanwhile, would I like to meet him at the Hitching Post on Hollywood

Boulevard at nine A.M. on Saturday? He said I should bring at least a dollar.

The other letter was from Melvin the shaman. It was on notepaper with kittens. Printed in pencil it said: *Sandor Eucalyptus may be in Los Angeles. Be careful. Trust no one. Your friend, Melvin the Shaman.*

"I have decided to major in drama," Eloise said.

CHAPTER 26

Hitching Post

I got to the Hitching Post movie theater at 8:50 A.M. Seamus was there. He was wearing my engineer's hat. I was wearing his cowboy hat. There was a huge mob of kids milling around on the sidewalk.

"Neddie!" Seamus Finn said. "You showed up!"

The kids who had bought their tickets were sort of surging up against the doors, which were locked. Seamus and I paid our thirty-five cents at the little box office, and surged too. When the doors were opened we sort of popped through and flowed into the lobby.

The Hitching Post was pretty similar to the Julian. The same shuffling of feet, the same low rumble of lots of kids talking and hollering, the same smell of popcorn and cinnamon red-hot candy, the same feeling of popcorn and spitwads bouncing off your head in the dark. First they showed a Farmer Gray cartoon, then a Flip the Frog, and a Porky Pig. Next came the serials, an episode apiece of *The Phantom Empire* and *The Fighting Devil Dogs*—both excellent. The feature films were *Wild Horse Valley* with Bob Steele, and *The Mask of Wu Shumai*. This movie had a villian, Dr. Wu Shumai, who was a genius and a master criminal. He wanted to steal this valuable jade frog because whoever had it could control the ancient underground gods, and take over the whole planet. This was an extremely good movie, with lots of scary stuff in it. Dr. Wu Shumai doesn't get the frog, but he gets away, and at the end of the movie there's a close-up, and he's looking right into the camera. He says, "You have not heard the last of Dr. Wu Shumai," and then he laughs a crazy evil laugh, and the last thing you see are his eyes.

When we came out of the Hitching Post, blinking in the sunlight, Seamus Finn said, "Let me show you the best place to get something to eat." He took me into a drugstore where a large root beer was a nickel and an order of french fries was fifteen cents. We shared the french fries, and put lots of catsup on them.

"Lunch for two for a quarter," Seamus said. "Best deal in town."

"That was a pretty good movie," I said. "Sort of reminded me of something."

"You mean how Dr. Wu Shumai was trying to get the jade frog, like Sandor Eucalyptus tried to get your turtle?" Seamus asked. "I was thinking the same thing."

"Do you think it's something like that? Do you think Sandor Eucalyptus is a master criminal and the turtle is some kind of magic?" I asked Seamus.

"I don't see how it could be anything else," Seamus Finn said.

"I got a letter from Melvin the shaman," I said. "He thinks Sandor Eucalyptus may be in Los Angeles. He said I should be careful and trust no one."

"I wish my father and Billy the Phantom Bellboy would come back," Seamus Finn said. "We could use some help. Meanwhile, we'll just have to deal with Sandor Eucalyptus ourselves."

"You don't think we should tell anyone? Like some adult?"

"He said trust no one, didn't he? Remember, in the movie, the police chief and the professor were in Dr. Wu Shumai's power. If we tell an adult, how do we know it won't be like that?"

Seamus had a point. Melvin the shaman had said to trust no one.

"I think we might tell Sergeant Caleb," Seamus said. "Sergeant Caleb is in nobody's power."

"Who's that?"

"He's a guy at the school. Let's walk over there now. I'll show you around, and you'll meet him. Did you decide to enroll?"

"Well, I think my father is willing to keep me out of school as long as I want—but he'd probably let me go if I asked. And my mother is all for me wearing a nice uniform and being polite. Let's look the place over."

CHAPTER 27

Old Pagoda

While we walked, Seamus Finn told me about the Brown-Sparrow Military Academy.

"One of our buildings is a six-hundred-year-old Japanese pagoda," he said. "It's the oldest building in California. These two brothers, the Hergeshleimers, were rich men who collected art from Asia. Around 1911 they decided to build a Japanese temple, a big one, to live in and keep all their art in. They brought lots of carpenters and sculptors and stonemasons from Japan and had the thing built right here in Hollywood—also all kinds of gardens, pools, and waterfalls. For good measure they had this actual fourteenth-century pagoda taken apart piece by piece and brought over here from Japan and put back together again.

"For a while, Hergeshleimers' Oriental Gardens was a big attraction. People came to see it, and take pictures of it, and get married in it. But by and by the brothers got tired of it, or got interested in something else, or died, or something, and the place started to get run down. After a while, it was more or less abandoned. People came and stole most of the statues, and pried some of the carvings off the buildings. The gardens went wild, and the whole place was covered with weeds and rotting away.

"Then these two retired movie actors, Brown and Sparrow, bought it, and turned it into a military school. They stuccoed over the main buildings and put up columns and sort of colonial doorways and windows, so it looked less like a Japanese temple and more like regular buildings such as you'd expect to find at a fancy private school. The old pagoda, however, survived pretty much intact, and looks like what it is. There's a classroom in it. Naturally, it's haunted like crazy. The Japanese ghosts are a whole different order of thing from ghosts like Billy the Phantom Bellboy and the ghosts around the Hermione Hotel. They don't just appear and fade away. They do a lot of wailing and screeching and gnashing of teeth and rushing at you. Anyway, that was what I was told. Nobody sees them much."

CHAPTER 28

Old School

If you didn't know it had once been a Japanese temple, Brown-Sparrow Military Academy would look to you like some college in New England. But there were some little giveaways, like the ends of the roofs turning up, and one or two dragons partially visible through the ivy on the walls.

The main gate had turned-up ends too, and was painted orange. Standing guard was a guy in a sharp, sharp, sharp marine uniform. Indian-looking guy, not tall, not short, not young, not old, not handsome, not ugly—just this guy in a crisp uniform with extra-good posture and white gloves.

"That looks like Melvin the shaman!" I said to Seamus Finn.

"It's Sergeant Caleb," Seamus Finn said. "He's the military guy in this school, and he knows everything. He was a real marine. The men teachers all have military titles and wear officers' uniforms, but they're just teachers. A lot of them were bit players in the movies—my father remembers some of them."

Sergeant Caleb snapped to attention. "Finn," he said. It's all last names at Brown-Sparrow.

"This is my friend Neddie Wentworthstein, Sergeant Caleb," Seamus said. "I'm going to show him around the school."

Sergeant Caleb produced a clipboard and a pencil.

"Write down your guest's name, Finn," he said.

"Excuse me, Sergeant Caleb," I said. "I just have to mention this—you remind me strongly of an Indian shaman I met in Albuquerque, New Mexico."

"You must mean Melvin—am I right?" Sergeant Caleb said.

"So you know him!" I said.

"Well, let's say the resemblance has been pointed out in the past," Sergeant Caleb said. "Enjoy your visit to Brown-Sparrow, Mr. Wentworthstein."

"Thank you," I said.

"If there's anything you need, feel free to call on me," Sergeant Caleb said. "And take care of that turtle."

As we walked away from the orange gate, I asked Seamus Finn, "How did he know about the turtle?"

"He knows about everything. I told you," Seamus Finn said.

The first thing I noticed about Brown-Sparrow was that it was fairly deserted. Now and then we saw a kid or two, mostly high schoolers, nobody around our age. The kids we saw were polite and said hello or smiled, but there was no one Seamus appeared to know very well.

"What's the deal? Where are all the kids?" I asked.

"Cadets. You have to call them cadets," Seamus Finn said. "It's the weekend. Most of the kids go home to their parents', unless their parents are too far away."

"Like yours."

"Well, my father is always off shooting a movie somewhere," Seamus Finn said. "And my mother lives in the East. I see her for a while in the summer, and sometimes she comes here."

"So you get lonely," I said.

"Sometimes another cadet invites me home for the weekend, but usually they just want to spend a lot of time alone with their families, so it's not very often. Probably, if you came here, you'd be a day cadet."

"Day cadet?"

"Not stay here at night. I mean, the Hermione is so close. You could walk here in less than ten minutes," Seamus said.

"And you could come and hang out with my family, weekends," I said. "We could explore the old hotel, maybe see the ghosts, and there's a pool. When I lived in Chicago, there were kids over all the time."

"I think you should be a day cadet," Seamus Finn said. "The dorm isn't that much fun. They make you clean your room constantly, and they tell you when to go to sleep, and you can't go to the kitchen and fix a snack like normal people."

"Sometimes my father and I have cornflakes late at night," I said.

"My father too," Seamus said.

The Brown-Sparrow Military Academy was a far cry from the Louis B. Nettelhorst School. It looked like a fancy private school such as you might see in the movies, and it was—a fancy private school, and also in the movies. Seamus told me that studios would come and do location shots from time to time. Some of the movie stars' kids who went there had been known to watch their movie star parents acting right outside their classroom windows.

Seamus showed me the classrooms, which were weirdly small—only ten or twelve cadets in a class.

He showed me the dorm rooms, which were weirdly clean and neat. There was the ancient pagoda, of course, in one corner of the parade ground. It was impressive. We peeked inside, but no Japanese ghosts rushed at us. There was a big gym, and a big indoor swimming pool, and the mess hall where everybody ate—it was big and fancy.

"How's the food here?" I asked.

"What do you care? You'd only be eating lunch here. You like Spam?" Seamus Finn asked.

"I don't think I've ever had Spam," I said.

"We have it often," Seamus Finn said.

"Speaking of such things," I said, "would you care to come back to the Hermione for supper?"

"Without making arrangements first?" Seamus Finn asked. "Without asking? Would it be all right?"

"Oh, it will be fine," I said. "I bring people home all the time. Besides, my parents like you. They'll be happy to see you."

"I'll tell Sergeant Caleb I'm going to be at your house," Seamus said. "Saturday is a Spam night."

CHAPTER 29

Family Life

Lettuce and tomato salad, hamburgers, mashed potatoes, spinach, and hot rolls. From the way Seamus Finn
carried on, you'd have thought it was caviar and lob-
sters. He even got all excited, and clapped his hands,
over the cherry Jell-O with green grapes in it for
dessert.

"I thought something light for dessert, because
we might stop for ice cream after the movies," my
mother said. "I thought we'd all go to the movies. Of
course, Seamus, you are welcome to come with us.
What time do you have to be back at the school?"

"I have to be in my room and in bed with the
lights out at nine, ma'am," Seamus said. My mother

loved when he called her ma'am. "Unless I was to stay overnight, of course."

"We'd be happy to have you stay, Seamus," my father said. "But I suppose we would need official permission from your father."

"Oh, my father has already informed the school that I am allowed to spend weekends with you, sir," Seamus Finn said. "And I told Sergeant Caleb this was where I would be."

"Your father told the school?" my father asked.

"Yes, he says you are the finest people he has ever met, and he trusts you completely," Seamus Finn said.

"I could make up the chaise longue on Neddie's porch as a bed," my mother said. "I think Seamus would be quite comfortable there."

"Let's look at the newspaper and see what movies are playing," my father said.

"Waffles for breakfast tomorrow," I whispered to Seamus.

Seamus Finn helped my mother clear the table and offered to dry the dishes. He was now a complete hit with her. She kissed him on the head.

"Roger," she said, "I think on Monday we should talk to the people at Brown-Sparrow. You'd like to go to school with Seamus, wouldn't you, Neddie?"

"You know, Mrs. Wentworthstein, there would

be a considerable savings if Neddie went to Brown-Sparrow as a day cadet," Seamus Finn said. "You live so conveniently nearby. And though I love the school, I have to say, the dorms are a little depressing."

"They are? Well, you are welcome to stay with us whenever you like," my mother said.

Seamus gave me the thumbs-up sign.

When you go out at night in Los Angeles you always see these white beams of light—searchlights aimed up at the sky. They have them when a new movie opens, or a supermarket, or a gas station, or for no reason in particular. You can always see three or four somewhere in the distance, moving around.

We drove out to the Cathay Circle Theater, which had two searchlights outside. It was another fancy movie house, not as spectacular as Grauman's Chinese, but still impressive. We saw *Romance on the High Seas*, a comedy with lots of music, and *The Sword of Caravaggio*, starring guess who. Even though his father was in it, Seamus said he had never seen the movie. Or he might have just been being polite. He was working the politeness for all he was worth—with results. It had gotten him what my parents still believed were unlimited weekend sleepovers. I knew he was moving in full-time. This was fine with me. I had always wished I had a brother instead of Eloise. Eloise, surprisingly, appeared to like Seamus too. She actually noticed him, and spoke to him. She had never paid the least attention to any friend of mine, or, most of the time, me.

The movies, the third and fourth feature-length ones we'd seen that day, not counting the serials and cartoons at the Hitching Post and the Bugs Bunny at the Cathay Circle, were fairly good. Aaron Finn did some pretty nice fencing in *The Sword of Caravaggio,* and the other movie had Doris Day, who is a good singer. After the movies we went to one of those places where you eat in your car, and had hot fudge sundaes.

CHAPTER 30

I'm a Cadet

My uniform cost $450! Two shirts, two pairs of wool serge pants with a black stripe up the sides, a dress uniform jacket, an overseas cap for daily wear, a garrison cap for wear with the dress uniform, an official Brown-Sparrow Windbreaker, a wool topcoat, a black necktie with built-in permanent knot, a web belt with brass Brown-Sparrow buckle. Also brass collar insignia that spelled out BSMA for wear with the shirts, brass lapel insignia for the dress uniform jacket, two spelling out BS and two with the school mascot, a little sparrow, a brass cap badge, and a brass shield for the garrison cap. The shirts had brass buttons with the little sparrow on them. Shoes we had to buy in a store—military-style five-eyelet oxfords (with

Wentworthstein military-grade shoelaces, of course). All the clothing was made to order by the school tailor, who had a shop right on the premises for making uniforms, doing repairs, cleaning, and pressing. Along with my uniform, I got a little booklet with instructions for taking care of everything, diagrams showing exactly where to pin the insignia, and a Blitz cloth for polishing the buttons, badges, and buckle. My father said it was the best-made suit of clothes he had ever seen, and ought to be for all that money.

While my uniform was being made, I spent my time in the school library, taking tests. I took four days of tests. These tests were fun—they were designed to find out how smart I was, how much I knew, and what grade I should be in. Various lady teachers and librarians brought me the tests, explained the tests, timed me, told me when to stop writing, collected the tests, and took them away to score. In between, I was free to read anything I wanted. I read a novel about a boy who went to a prep school and wanted to be a football hero at Yale, a book about reptiles and amphibians of California, with special attention to turtles, and a book all about etiquette and good manners. I paid a lot of attention to that book. I figured the more polite I could make myself, the better I would do in my new school.

Lunchtimes, I would walk to the mess hall and eat with the two librarians, Mrs. Coburn and Mrs. Steele. Every cadet had an assigned place to eat at a table with the same other cadets at every meal—and I hadn't been assigned one yet. In the afternoons, Cadet Sergeant Winkler, a high school kid, took me to the parade ground when no one was using it and taught me how to march, salute, and do the manual of arms. The manual of arms is all the things you do with a fake rifle, and I learned right-shoulder arms, left-shoulder arms, order arms, and things like that. I had to do everything snappily and crisply. I am not a snappy or crisp person by nature, but Cadet Sergeant Winkler was a good teacher, and yelled at me a lot. It was fun, in a way.

At the end of the week, Colonel Groscase, the commandant—the head military guy—came out and watched Cadet Sergeant Winkler put me through my paces. He said we had both done a good job.

On Friday, I took my uniform home with me. I also took Seamus Finn home with me. He was a big help. He showed me how to cut a slit in a piece of cardboard and slide it behind each button so the Blitz cloth wouldn't get your shirt greasy—and there's a lot of technique involved with shoe-polishing.

On Monday we went to school early so Seamus

could go to his dorm room and put his uniform on. I reported to the office of Major Grey, the headmaster, the head academic guy. I was looking snappy and crisp, with everything shiny. Major Grey looked exactly like George Washington, and I knew he had played him in two movies, because Seamus had told me. He was a nice man with kind eyes. He told me all my tests had been evaluated and he would take me to meet my teacher and my classmates.

My teacher was Miss Magistra. She was a small woman with a sharp nose and quick dark eyes. Like most of the lady teachers, she was on the old side. What Seamus Finn had told me was that the lady teachers, which is to say most of the teachers for first through eighth grades, had retired from teaching in regular schools before coming to teach at Brown-Sparrow. This meant that they all had about thirty years of experience, and had seen everything. This may have been more true of Miss Magistra, who was rumored not only to have retired from the public schools of Baton Rouge, Louisiana, but also to have been acquitted of shooting someone in a gambling hall. It was also thought that Magistra was not her real name.

"Class, this is Wentworthstein," Miss Magistra said. "Wentworthstein will be joining us, and I know you will all make him welcome. Cadet Wentworth-stein, these are cadets Terwilliger, Larabee, Burns, Stover, Finn, Crane, Merriwell, McCoy, and Henderson."

Each kid stood and made a little bow when Miss Magistra spoke his name. Seamus Finn also flashed me a smile. The cadets looked reasonably intelligent and pleasant. Of course, I had already had a rundown on the members of my class from my friend Seamus. No bullies, no snitches, no crybabies, no showoffs—a pretty good bunch, he thought.

CHAPTER 31

I'm Learning

Something Seamus Finn had not mentioned to me was that our class was studying paleontology for this year's science topic! What a stroke of luck! Although I had a general idea from reading the signs at the La Brea Tar Pits, and my book from the drugstore, there was still quite a bit I wasn't clear about, and I really wanted to know all about fossils, and evolution, and geologic periods.

Right there, on my very first day in class, I got it straight. Well, straighter—there's a lot to remember. First there are eons, which are really long, like millions and millions and millions of years. There's the Pre-Archean, the Archean, the Proterozoic, and the Phanerozoic. When the name of an eon ends in "zoic," that means there was animal life—and we know about that from fossils. The eons are divided up into eras, which are also millions and millions of years, but not quite as many. Eras are divided into periods—for example, the Mesozoic era, which is neat because dinosaurs lived then, is divided up into the Triassic, the Jurassic, and the Cretaceous. And then the periods are divided into epochs, like Early Jurassic, Middle Jurassic, and Late Jurassic.

My favorite epoch, because it's when the tar pits were sucking down animals, is the Pleistocene, which is the first part of the Quaternary period, which took place in the Cenozoic era, and it's practically now, because it happened up until about 8,000 years ago, and belongs in the Phanerozoic eon, which started around 600,000,000 years ago, and we're still living in it.

Miss Magistra had a nifty chart on the wall with different colors showing all this stuff, also some actual fossils from the Cambrian, Silurian, and Devonian periods—mostly little bugs and shellfish-type critters—plus lots of pictures of dinosaurs, and mammoths, the sort of extinct animals anybody would like.

Apparently the class was going to take a field trip to the tar pits, and also go someplace where we could dig for fossils—and these things had not taken place yet. So I had come to the school at just the right time.

While I was learning things, I was also trying to size up my classmates. I couldn't learn much. Everybody was interested in the science lesson, and mostly knew the answers to questions Miss Magistra asked. Nobody said or did anything outstanding. I thought I'd probably get to talk to them when lunchtime came around.

CHAPTER 32

I'm Eating

When the bell rang for lunch, nobody did anything until Miss Magistra said, "Class, rise." Then we all stood by our desks, at attention. "Dismissed," she said, and we all walked out of the classroom and down the hall, nobody talking. I just followed along.

"Just follow along," Cadet Finn whispered to me. We went out of the building and to the parade ground.

Cadet Sergeant Winkler was looking for me. "Wentworthstein, you are in the third squad of the second platoon of Company B. You stand here, between Burns and Stover. This is your place whenever we are in formation."

Then, a long way off, someone hollered, "Battalion!" and immediately someone a little closer hollered,

"Company!" and Cadet Second Lieutenant Shmedlap hollered, "Platoon!" Then the same bunch of voices all hollered, "Ten-shun!" And we all snapped to attention. Then right face, and forward march, and the Brown-Sparrow band started playing. It was a really good band. The band was formed outside the mess hall, and we marched there while it played, up the steps, and in the door. Then everybody went to stand behind his seat. Cadet Sergeant Winkler showed me where to stand and told me this was where I was always to sit. Someone hollered, "Be seated," and we all sat down.

It wasn't over. We sat at attention. Nobody talked, and we all had to hold our arms out in front of us, folded one over the other Indian-style, until someone hollered, "At ease." Sitting at the head of our table was Cadet Second Lieutenant Shmedlap, who said, "Gentlemen, you may now talk quietly while you enjoy your Spam."

Spam is disgusting. It's some kind of canned meat. It's rectangular. They fry it. We also had warmish shredded carrot salad with raisins, bread and butter, and milk that could have been colder. Dessert was . . . dessert. It was slightly sweet. It might have been cake, or it might have been pudding. Now I understood why Seamus Finn had gotten all excited about hamburgers and mashed potatoes.

CHAPTER 33

I'm Talking

I looked around the mess hall at the whole school having lunch. All the tables were set up like mine, with a cadet officer, a high schooler, at the head, and lower ranks or younger kids in the other seats. All the cadets looked similar, not just because we were all dressed exactly alike—everybody had the same sort of facial expressions, moved the same way, had the same sort of haircut. I couldn't quite put my finger on what it was, this similarity. Terwilliger, one of the cadets in my class, and at my table, explained it.

"Everybody here is rich," he said. There were more kinds of kids than I had known at the Louis B. Nettelhorst School. By more kinds I mean from more places—about a quarter of the cadets were Jewish.

There were quite a few Chinese kids, and Filipinos, kids from Mexico and other places in Latin America. "Brown-Sparrow would take a Negro," Terwilliger said, "if his father was rich enough, and he didn't mind being the only black kid in school."

Rich people look different from other people. This was something I had never noticed before. Of course, I was rich myself, being the son of the shoelace king—but this was the first time I had ever really thought about it.

All the other cadets at my table knew that my father was Wentworthstein shoelaces. They knew about my trip on the Super Chief, and about me being left behind in Flagstaff, Arizona, and being friends with Seamus Finn and his father, the movie actor. Seamus Finn, who did not sit at my table, had told a couple of his friends in the dorm, and they had discussed me with the others. They knew all about me before I ever came to the school.

What they wanted to tell me about at that first lunch was who their fathers were, and that they were rich—which went without saying, really, because they were there—what sports they were good at, and places they had been on vacations. What they wanted to know about me was what sports I was good at (none, really), whether my sister was pretty (yes, but too old for any of them), and didn't I agree that I was a lucky boy to be going to such a swell school.

They were friendly and polite, and seemed more grown-up than the kids I'd gone to school with in Chicago. I found I was missing those kids, and I wondered what Ronnie Wolfspit was doing. It was a swell school, and I already liked Miss Magistra, and I was excited that I was going to learn more about paleontology, and probably other stuff, in her class—but I felt a little lonely for the first time since I'd left home.

The only kid at my table I especially liked was Cadet Junior Private Crane, Alfred, a nice-looking boy, on the small side, who sat across from me, and was also in Miss Magistra's class. He was the only one who didn't brag about his father, or say very much of anything—but he looked as though he was fighting back a smile, and his eyes twinkled when the other kids were talking.

CHAPTER 34

Stuffed Stuff

I had been going to Brown-Sparrow for a couple of weeks, and was fairly used to it, on the day Seamus Finn and I ran into Crane at the Safeway. My mother had sent us to get two cans of sauerkraut, some Chinese noodles, and a bag of miniature marshmallows for her tuna casserole. Seamus was staying for supper. He had not missed a single supper with us and came over for breakfast on those mornings when he had not actually slept over.

"I say, Crane!" Seamus said.

"Call me Al," Crane said. "We're not in school." Crane was a day cadet like me, and like Seamus, for all intents and purposes. "I'm just picking up a couple of things for my mom."

"That's what we're doing," Seamus said. "For our mom—I mean, his mom."

"I'm going to get a root beer. Want to share it?" Al asked. We paid for our purchases, including a twelve-ounce bottle of Dad's Old Fashioned Root Beer from the cooler, and went outside. We put our grocery bags on the fender of a parked car and stood around taking turns sipping.

Al Crane was different out of his uniform and away from school. He seemed easier and friendlier—not that he seemed unfriendly at school, just that he talked less than anyone else. "You guys have to be home right away?" he asked.

"Not particularly," I said.

"You ever been in here?" he said, indicating the store next to the Safeway. It had a big glass window with venetian blinds going all the way across. The blinds were angled down and you couldn't see inside. There was no sign like most stores have, just a small card I'd never noticed before on the glass door. STUFFED STUFF 'N' STUFF was typed on the card.

"What is it? It looks like an office or something," I said.

"It's a neat place. We can go in. Come on," Al Crane said.

"But what is it?" Seamus asked.

"You'll see. Come on."

We picked up our grocery bags and followed Al to the door. It was unlocked. We followed him in.

The first thing I saw was an African lion, about one foot from my nose. I jumped. Seamus had the same reaction. It only took a second to realize that it was stuffed and not alive—but you can go through quite a number of emotions in one second. The emotion I settled on was that it was an extremely neat thing.

We began taking in the rest of the room. It was large and slightly dim, and there were a lot of stuffed animals, including a rhino and a giraffe. There were also glass cases, and tables and shelves and counters with all kinds of things on them. There was a doorway at the back, which probably led to an office or work-room.

We heard a voice from the doorway. "Who goes there?" it shouted.

"It's Al," Al shouted back. "Okay if my friends and I look around?"

"Sure," the voice said. "I'm just packing up an alligator. I'll be with you in a few minutes."

We looked around at the things in the room. There were lots of stuffed animals, and animal heads, birds, a cobra about to strike, and fish—also primitive-looking carvings, suits of medieval armor, Indian beadwork such as I had seen in Albuquerque, old-fashioned hats, rusty pistols, and swords.

A guy with a beard came out of the back room.

"This is Steve Kraft," Al said. "Steve, these are my friends, Seamus and Neddie."

"What sort of place is this?" Seamus asked.

"It's my shop," Steve Kraft said. "I have taxidermics, curios, and antiquities. I have taxidermied fauna—that's animals—like this bandicoot here. I also have antiquities, like this Siamese Buddha, medical anomalies, like this two-headed bunny in formaldehyde, and, as you see in this case, bottlecaps, and over here, beer cans."

"What do you do, sell them?" I asked.

"Sometimes I sell them. Very often I rent them to the movie studios—they are shooting a picture about the Middle Ages, I provide suits of armor. They're shooting a scene in a Chinese temple, I provide authentic, or nearly authentic, carvings and decorations. Some of my customers are collectors like myself. And some things I just keep for me." Steve Kraft lowered his voice to a whisper: "Except for some of the animals, everything in the place is fake—I make it myself. For example, this is the head of a leper, made of wax. Scary, isn't it? I made that from scratch. Most of the better exhibits are made from molds. I make a rubber mold, let's say of a skull, and then I cast it in plaster or plastic and paint it."

Seamus and I were gaping, mouths open. This was the neatest thing of its kind I had seen yet. It beat the store on Hollywood Boulevard with the magic tricks and models and switchblades. I don't like to admit it, because the Indian Building was obviously more important, and more real, but I liked this better than the Indian Building. It even beat the La Brea Tar Pits in some ways.

"I have fossils too," Steve Kraft said. "This is the skull of a dire wolf, from the tar pits. Notice how the bone is black and the teeth are white? That's because the bone absorbed the asphalt, and the teeth, being much less porous, didn't. Completely fake, of course— it's made of plastic. All the real ones are in the county museum. But it's good, isn't it?"

Al Crane was grinning proudly at how impressed Seamus and I were. Seamus tugged my sleeve. "Look at this," he whispered. In a glass case was my turtle! I mean, it was exactly like my turtle.

"Uh, what is this little item, Mr. Kraft?" Seamus asked.

"Sacred turtle," Steve Kraft said. "Naturally, I mean a fake sacred turtle. A real one, if anybody could get it, would be priceless. I copied this from a picture in an old book. It's really carved out of fake stone I make by mixing sand and vermiculite with plaster. Then I painted it."

"It's really good," I said. "I mean, it looks just like a real one."

"Nobody's ever seen a real one," Steve Kraft said. "There may only be one real one, and nobody knows where it is—but a Jesuit priest who was friends with an Indian shaman drew a picture of it more than a hundred years ago, and that's what I copied."

"Do you know what it's supposed to mean?" I asked, trying to sound mildly curious.

"Very sacred thing," Steve Kraft said. "It figures into the most secret rituals of just about every Indian tribe, also South American Indians, and Pacific Island types, and Asians, and Africans. Sacred animal everywhere, I guess. The Anishnabe say the seven parts of the turtle—the head, tail, shell, and four legs—stand for the seven codes of life: bravery, respect, honesty, humility, wisdom, honor, and sharing. Only a hero can possess the sacred turtle, and he has to defeat powerful forces of evil, or the world will cease to exist."

"Would you sell this turtle?" Seamus asked.

"No, I would never sell it," Steve Kraft said. "It's one of the best things I've ever faked."

Back outside, on the street in front of Stuffed

Stuff 'n' Stuff, Al Crane asked us, "What are you guys doing on Saturday?"

"Probably catch the movies at the Hitching Post," Seamus said.

"I live right across the street from the Hitching Post," Al Crane said. "If you want, you could come with me to see where my father works."

"Would that be fun?" I asked.

"Yes, he works in an interesting place, and it's out in the country among the farms. We'd get to take a car ride, and lunch will be memorable."

"What does your father do?" Seamus asked.

"He's a manager. He's a business manager. He's nice, and my mother is nice too. Want to come?"

"Sure, we'll keep you company," I said.

"Yes, it will be nice to go for a ride," Seamus said.

"Great. Tell your parents you'll be gone all day," Al Crane said.

CHAPTER 35

He Saw What I Did

"I saw what you did," Seamus Finn said as the two of us walked back to the Hermione.

"The French substitution? Did I do it right? Do you think Kraft saw it?" I asked.

"No, you did it perfectly," Seamus said. "The only reason I saw it was because I was looking for it. I was thinking it would be the right thing to do."

"So you agree it was a good idea to switch the real turtle with Steve Kraft's fake one?"

"I think it's a perfect hiding place. No one would look for it in a shop full of fakes. Steve Kraft is obviously a friendly guy—we can go in there anytime we want and do a reverse substitution. And he said he would never sell it," Seamus Finn said. "So it's just as safe as if it were in a bank vault."

"Now I can stop worrying that Sandor Eucalyptus will catch up with me and pick my pocket, or pull a gun on me," I said. "What do you think about that stuff about a hero defeating the powers of evil and the world ceasing to exist?"

"Well, legends always have stuff like that in them," Seamus said. "It sounds good. But there's obviously something magical about the turtle, and Melvin the shaman did give it to you."

"He also said to take care of it," I said. "I wonder if that meant I should keep it on my person, or just keep it safe. I took a chance that he meant to keep it safe—and I think it's safer where I put it."

"We could ask Sergeant Caleb for an opinion," Seamus Finn said. "He already knows about the turtle. You want to do that?"

"No, I think I did the right thing," I said. "Let's keep it between ourselves, and trust no one."

CHAPTER 36

A Car Ride

Saturday morning, outside the Hitching Post, Al Crane asked us, "Well, what's it going to be? The movies, or are you coming with us?"

"You asked us every day at school," I said. "We're coming with you."

"Great!" Al said. "Come up to the apartment. I'll show you my stuff and you can meet my parents. We'll be leaving soon."

We went across the street, through a little door, and up a flight of stairs. Al's apartment was above the shoe store. He had an excellent collection of comics, and some good model airplanes. There were lots of paintings of clowns on all the walls. His parents were friendly—father sort of fat, and mother sort of thin.

"Have you had your breakfast, boys?" Mrs. Crane asked.

We had, but she insisted we have a doughnut apiece anyway.

"I'm bringing some comics to read in the car," Al said.

"Let's roll. Time's a-wasting," Al's father said.

It was a big green sedan. There was plenty of room in the back, and the three of us read comics, looked out the windows, punched one another, and made funny noises, while Al's mother and father talked to each other in the front seat. It was a nice day, and we were driving way out in the country. We were all in a good mood.

We got into an area where there were nice-looking little farms, barns, fenced fields, little farmhouses, some cattle here and there, and horses. "We'll be there pretty soon," Al said.

"To where your father works," I said.

"Right," Al said.

"It's a farm?" I asked.

"Sort of."

I was looking at a neat farmhouse, white with a red roof, and grazing next to it, where you might see a cow or a donkey, was a llama. I was just going to mention that when Al's father turned the car into the long driveway. In the distance, I saw a couple of camels.

"We're here!" Al said.

"Where your father works," I said.

"Right."

"Is that an elephant?" I asked.

"That's Big Louise," Al said.

"This is where your father works?"

"Yes."

"As a business manager?"

"Right."

"Of?"

"Of the Gibbs Brothers Circus," Al said. "The second-biggest circus in the world. This is the winter quarters—they keep all the animals here and train them up for the season. Circuses only travel in the summertime."

Seamus Finn had an expression of complete surprise and complete happiness. I must have looked the same way.

Mr. Crane pulled the car up in front of the farmhouse. "Okay, boys, we're turning you loose. Listen for the lunch bell, and don't upset the animals too much."

"Let's go and see if they're working with the cats," Al said. "I like the cats best."

Al led us to a big cage, as big as a basketball court. Inside there was a guy wearing blue jeans and a T-shirt, with a pistol in a holster, holding a whip—and eight lions.

"That's Fred, the assistant lion tamer," Al said. "Of course, in the show the lion act is done by Clive Montague. Fred does the training, though. It's not really taming—they're wild lions—he just trains them."

"Oh, hi, Al," Fred said. He walked up to the bars and Al introduced us. The lions were all sitting on drum-shaped platforms. "How are you doing at school? See my new lion over there? This is his first week. His name is Ferdinand."

While Al was talking with us through the bars, one of the lions dropped down off his platform and came across the cage, fast, right at Fred. Before any of us could say a word, Fred spun around, pulled out his pistol, and fired a shot. The lion stopped. Fred cracked his whip. "Get back up there, Ferdinand," he said in a calm, friendly voice. Ferdinand looked confused. Fred took a step toward him. Ferdinand took a step back. "Be a good boy—get on your perch," Fred said. Ferdinand did it.

"It's blanks in the gun," Al said. "Just to get their attention. And he never hits them with the whip either, just pops it."

"I have to get back to work, boys," Fred said. "I'll see you at lunch. Hang around if you like."

Seamus Finn and I were in a state of extreme joy. Also amazement. The amazement was mostly at Al Crane. Here he was in a school where everybody was the son of a big shot and all they did was brag about their fathers. Crane was the only kid whose father actually had a job anyone would be impressed by, and he never said anything about it. We knew without his saying anything that we were not to mention any of this when we got back to Brown-Sparrow.

"Hey, is that Al?" someone was shouting. "If you have a minute, come over here and help me out! Bring those other kids with you." It was Bobby, the elephant trainer, big fat guy, sort of like an elephant himself. After introductions were made, he explained what he wanted. "I need riders. It would be a big help if you kids would ride these elephants for me. If you don't mind."

We didn't mind. Al knew all about how to ride, and how to steer, an elephant—and he showed Seamus and me what to do.

"Just take them all around the farm," Bobby said. "Practice right turns and left turns, and backing up. Don't let them get away with anything—they'll take advantage of you if they can."

My elephant's name was Sadie, and while she was lifting me up onto her head, with her trunk under my sneaker, I had a look into her wise brown eye and fell deeply and forever in love. She fell in love with me at the same moment. I don't know how I knew that, but I did. It's that way with elephants and a lot of animals. They know right away if you're a friend of theirs. I spent that morning being in the one place on earth I wanted to be, swaying on top of Sadie, telling her to go left and right and back—and she was just as happy as I was, moving through the fields of the Gibbs Brothers Circus winter quarters. Al told me later that if I didn't see Sadie for another ten years, she would remember me, and we would still be friends whenever we met again.

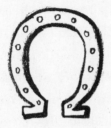

CHAPTER 37

Death

We had lunch in the farmhouse. All the trainers and animal keepers and farm workers were there, along with Al's mother and father, and us three kids. There was a big kitchen, with a long table, and that's where we ate. The cook, Miss Mildred, had been a circus cook for fifty years, and she was great. There must have been fifteen or twenty different dishes, plus three kinds of pie, and everything was good. All the workers were strong-looking guys, and they disussed how the training was going, and told stories about the animals. Some of them had really neat scars, and they told about how they had gotten them. I sort of wished I had a scar from being clawed by a tiger or a bear.

"You know, I work with the circus in the summertime," Al said. "I get paid and everything."

Seamus and I admired Al like crazy. He had the best life of any kid we had ever heard of.

At the end of the meal, the men wandered off, back to work, and Al took Seamus and me out to see more things around the place. We saw a couple of guys leading a nice old brown horse. They took it down into a little pasture with a tree in the middle. Under the tree, one of them took out a pistol, and shot the horse in the head! It pitched over, dead! I felt all cold and sweaty all of a sudden, and like I was going to lose my lunch. Seamus was looking white.

The men had picked up tools that were leaning against the tree and were busy cutting up the nice old horse that had been alive a couple of minutes ago.

My mouth was dry, and my voice sounded funny to me.

"They . . . killed that horse," I said.

"I don't like it either," Al said. "But what did you think lions eat? You want to go see them get fed?"

"Please, no," Seamus said. "I mean, no, thanks. Can we go hang out with the elephants some more?"

"Yes, can we do that?" I asked.

CHAPTER 38

It's a School

Brown-Sparrow seemed different after visiting the Gibbs Brothers Circus winter quarters with Al Crane. For one thing, I was more aware of the way Al was treated by the other cadets. Everybody was polite to everybody, and I can't say they were mean to him—but it was clear that he didn't count as much as some of the other kids, the ones whose fathers were famous movie stars, or big men in the movie studios, or just very rich. They didn't ask Al's opinion about things, or listen when he talked. It was subtle—the way they stood when he was around, sort of not making a space for him in the group. If I had asked anybody, they would have said he was a good kid, and they liked him, but I knew they didn't think he was very important.

It didn't seem to bother Al—but why would it? He rode elephants, and knew lion tamers, and worked in the circus. To him, the other cadets must have seemed fairly silly. Of course, neither Seamus nor I ever said a word about the circus, and keeping that secret made us separate from the other cadets, and being separate made us look at them slightly differently.

Then there was the military thing. The everybody-looking-alike thing. This went beyond looking sharp on the parade ground. There was a feeling you were supposed to be a certain kind of person.

I was all right, of course, because I was friends with Finn and his father was a big actor. But if it weren't for that, I thought, I would probably have been treated the same as Crane.

One of the kids in my class, Stover, said to me, "You know, they watch people like you." I didn't ask him what he meant—it just gave me an icky feeling. Stover was a corporal—the highest rank of anybody in our class. He was always kissing up to teachers, older cadets, higher ranks. I knew if he ever saw me breaking a rule he would turn me in. He was the one watching me. He knew that I could be a rule breaker.

I still liked the school. Miss Magistra was a good teacher, and class was always fun. I liked the marching and the military stuff too, especially the band.

Seamus was in the junior band, not the one that played on the parade ground—and he really wanted to get good enough to be promoted. The school had a great hobby shop in the basement, with all the tools anyone would want, and balsa wood, and glue, and plastic, and paint, all free of charge. Seamus and Al and I often spent time there after school, working on our model airplanes. There was even a hobby shop teacher, Mr. Resnek, the mechanical drawing teacher, a nice guy who was there from two to five every day and would help cadets with their projects.

Brown-Sparrow had a lot of good points. What I was realizing was that it just wasn't a warm and cuddly sort of place—but maybe that's how a military school is supposed to be.

The only other person, besides Seamus and Al, who seemed to understand my mixed feelings about the place was Sergeant Caleb, who I was pretty sure was really Melvin the shaman—only, how could he have been? Sometimes he would say things to me when I walked past his post at the gate, sort of as if he were breaking into my thoughts. "There are idiots wherever you go, Wentworthstein," he might say, out of a clear sky. Other times, he would say things like "Put your hat on straight, Wentworthstein" or "Don't slouch, Wentworthstein—you're walking like an armadillo."

CHAPTER 39

One Night at Home

"How are things going at school?" my father wanted to know.

"It's good. It's good, Dad. It's a good school."

"Neddie is doing well in class, and the cadets like him," Seamus Finn said. "I'll be happy to clean the parakeet cage after supper."

"You're a fine boy, Seamus," my mother said.

"I need you to sign a permission slip so I can be in a play," Eloise said.

"I found a new supermarket, just three blocks away," my mother said. "That's where I got these lamb chops."

We had gradually stopped being visitors and tourists and were simply a family living in Los

Angeles. My father had taken to going around and visiting shoelace dealers, and shoelace warehouses, and shoe stores that sold shoelaces. He had also made friends with a guy who worked for the costume department at one of the movie studios and specialized in authentic period and historical shoelaces—he had a sort of shoelace museum in his house, and owned a shoelace that had belonged to Robert E. Lee. My father had mentioned that maybe he would ask to borrow it, to put in a display case, if he should open a West Coast office of Wentworthstein Shoelaces.

My mother spent her days rearranging the furniture, buying things we needed, and talking to ladies she met at the market and around the Hermione Hotel. "There is a very nice family living here," she said. "They have a daughter who's Seamus and Neddie's age. I told them we would watch television with them in the lobby this evening."

There was a television set in the lobby of the Hermione. It was a fancy lobby, 1920s-style, with lots of comfortable furniture. The television set was coin operated—you dropped a quarter in the slot and got a half-hour. Back in Chicago, Ronnie Wolfspit's parents had gotten a television set shortly before we left, and several times we had been invited over to watch. Everybody sat in the living room and squinted at the little screen, and Ronnie Wolfspit's mother served snacks. It was the first television set I had seen in private hands, though I had seen one on a trip to a museum.

My father said that his friend in the movie business, the shoelace collector, had told him the studios were worried that with television catching on the way it was, the movies would go broke. I couldn't see that happening until someone invented a television with a screen bigger than ten inches.

CHAPTER 40

Watching TV with
the Birnbaums

When we went down to the lobby, the family my mother had met were already in place before the pay TV set. The mother was a neatly dressed little woman about my mother's age. The daughter looked to be the same age as Seamus and me, but taller—she had on a frilly dress, those black shoes that girls wear with the little strap that goes across, and a ribbon that went over the top of her head. She had blond hair, and she looked like one of those girls who thinks boys are icky, and cries a lot, and worries about getting her clothes dirty. The father was a good deal older than my father, had flowing white hair, and was really handsome. Seamus and I recognized him at once—it was Captain Buffalo Birnbaum, one of the great old-time cowboy actors! Captain Buffalo Birnbaum was the real McCoy—he had been a real cowboy, a real marshal, and an officer in the United States Cavalry, and he was a famous expert on Indian cultures and languages. Even Seamus, whose own father was a famous movie star, and who had grown up going to birthday parties at movie stars' houses, was impressed to meet Captain Buffalo Birnbaum.

"These are the Birnbaums," my mother said. "Nancy, Captain Buffalo, and little Yggdrasil." Yggdrasil is pronounced "Ig-druh-sil."

"Do people call you Iggy?" I asked little Yggdrasil.

"Yes, they do—once. Then I pop them in the nose. Care to give it a try, military school boy?" little Yggdrasil said.

Appearances can be deceiving.

"I think you may know my father," Seamus said to Captain Buffalo Birnbaum.

"Aaron Finn! I see the resemblance. I taught him to ride," Captain Buffalo Birnbaum said. "Nice young fellow." Captain Buffalo Birnbaum had a steely gaze, a straight nose, thin lips, and a powerful jaw. You got the impression that everything he said was true, and that if a grizzly bear suddenly appeared in the hotel lobby he would have dealt with it without breaking a sweat. "I've already fed the television a quarter," Captain Buffalo Birnbaum said to my father. "The next round is yours."

We settled down to watching. It was a variety program—people got up and sang, and there were comedy skits, and a lousy ventriloquist. I was bored in five minutes.

"This stinks," Yggdrasil Birnbaum said. "Come on," she said to Seamus and me. "Let's look around the hotel."

We left the grownups watching television and followed Yggdrasil to the back of the lobby, where there was a little door. It was locked. Yggdrasil looked over her shoulder and took a key out of her pocket. "This is a master key—it opens every door in the place," she said. She opened the door, and we slipped through, into a sort of utility space behind the lobby.

"We've lived here for years," Yggdrasil said. "This hotel is old. Used to be a hot address in the silent movie days, when my father first came to Hollywood. Now it's just apartments, so lots of it isn't used anymore. There are rooms and rooms closed up and nobody ever goes there. And it has ghosts. You have a problem with ghosts?"

"We have a personal friend who's a ghost," Seamus Finn said.

"I'll show you the restaurant," Yggdrasil Birn-baum said.

She led us down a hallway and unlocked another door. When Yggdrasil switched on the light, we saw a whole restaurant, with chairs and tables, and fancy chandeliers, and lots of fancy woodwork, weird-looking arches, and snakey-looking decorations. "It's Moorish," Yggdrasil said. "Moorish and Arabian stuff was a big fad. There was this movie where Rudolph Valentino played an Arab sheik—huge movie, and the whole country went crazy for this kind of decor. Valentino lived in this hotel. Sometimes I do my homework in here."

"What a neat place!" Seamus said.

"Isn't it?" Yggdrasil said.

Yggdrasil told us there was a second swimming pool, and tennis courts, out behind the hotel and hidden by weeds and bushes, and also a bowling alley.

"And there are secret rooms that got closed off when they remodeled. You have to go in through the windows. I might show you sometime. Also, I have a lot of fireworks hidden away—just waiting for the right time to set them off. But that's enough of you two for now. Let's go back and see what the adults are doing."

CHAPTER 41

Video Voodoo

They were into their second quarter's worth of viewing. Now the show was *Places and Faces Around L.A.* It was a program that dragged cameras and lights and cables to different locations and interviewed various interesting citizens. This time they were visiting Nick Bluegum, owner of Nick's Knickknackery on Pico Boulevard.

"Mr. Bluegum is not only the proprietor of one of Los Angeles's finest shops, specializing in curios, gifts, gimcracks, and objets d'art," the announcer was saying. "He is also a famous collector, and expert in ethnological artifacts and oddities." Nick Bluegum was an insane-looking character with a greasy mustache. He was wearing a dark suit and smiling into the camera.

"I find this interesting," Seamus Finn whispered to me.

"So do I," I whispered back.

"And why do you find it interesting?" he whispered.

"Because that guy reminds me of Sandor Eucalyptus," I whispered.

"Know what else?" Seamus Finn whispered.

"What?" I whispered.

"Know another name for a blue gum tree?" Seamus whispered.

"Eucalyptus?" I whispered.

"Shut up," Yggdrasil Birnbaum whispered. "You guys are distracting me with all the whispering."

Then something happened—or didn't happen—or seemed to happen . . . No, it happened, but it didn't happen in a normal way. Not normal at all. What happened was Nick Bluegum, who was talking with the TV announcer about his knickknack store and the things in his collection, at the same time—while he was talking to the guy—looked into the camera and said, "Nedward Wentworthstein, I want that turtle!" And I knew nobody else saw or heard him do or say that! But I also knew he had, and I had seen it and heard it.

"You look weird," Seamus Finn whispered. "Something happen?"

"We're going again," Yggdrasil said. "You two kids, come with me."

I was still in some kind of state of shock while Seamus and I left the lobby with Yggdrasil.

We were back in the restaurant. "What's going on with you two beach balls?" Yggdrasil asked.

"What makes you think something's going on?" Seamus asked.

"What? With the whispering, and Neddie going pale, I'd have to be an idiot. So, tell me what the deal is. I'm trustworthy, and besides, if you don't tell me, I might just thump it out of you."

"I don't know," I said to Seamus. "Should we tell her?"

"I'm going into the kitchen to make us all a hot chocolate," Yggdrasil said. "Talk it over, and when I come back, I want the story. Things are dull enough around here—if you guys are involved in something interesting, I want in."

"Is this hot chocolate left over from the golden age of the movies?" I asked.

"It's instant. I keep packets here. I have powdered chicken soup too. You want?"

Yggdrasil went into the kitchen at the back of the defunct restaurant.

"She's pretty bossy," Seamus said.

"Yes, but it might be good to have her on our side if we have to fight or anything."

"Plus, we're scared of her," Seamus said. "Let's take a chance and tell her."

When Yggdrasil Birnbaum came back with three cups of ghastly instant hot chocolate, Seamus and I told her about Melvin the shaman giving me the turtle, and Sandor Eucalyptus trying to get it from me, and jumping out of the airplane, and Melvin the shaman's letter to me saying that Sandor Eucalyptus was in Los Angeles, and the fake sacred turtle at Stuffed Stuff 'n' Stuff, and how I had switched the real one with it, and then Nick Bluegum appearing on television and giving me a secret message that no one else had seen.

"Cool!" Yggdrasil said. "Come with me."

We went back to the lobby. The grownups had let the television set go off and were sitting around talking.

"Excuse me, Dad," Yggdrasil said to Captain Buffalo Birnbaum. "What do you know about a sacred turtle, one made out of stone?"

"Sacred turtle. Very important artifact. There are lots of them around, but only one real one—and that's been lost for ages. When I lived with the Paiutes, they said that the one and only real sacred turtle came from a long way off, had serious magical powers, and in the right hands could prevent the destruction of the world. In the wrong hands, hoo-boy! Let me think— what else do I know about it? Oh, yes, it is made of stone, but not igneous stone, and not sedimentary stone, and not metamorphic stone."

Seamus and I knew what he was talking about because we studied geology in Miss Magistra's class. "Aren't those all the kinds of rocks there are on the planet?" I asked.

"So I believe, but the article isn't made of any of them. Draw your own conclusions," Captain Buffalo Birnbaum said. "Why do you ask, daughter?"

"No reason. We were just talking," Yggdrasil Birnbaum said.

CHAPTER 42

We Get Organized

Yggdrasil had told Seamus and me to skip breakfast the next day, which was Sunday, and meet her in the lobby. "Bring money," she said.

"Sunday is waffles at our house—I mean, Neddie's house," Seamus said.

"It's fried eggplant and venison at mine," Yggdrasil said. "So I breakfast out. You can treat me."

She was waiting in the lobby when we came downstairs. We went to the Rolling Doughnut, shaped like a doughnut, naturally, on Vine Street, where she ordered hot doughnuts and coffee for the three of us. "My friends are paying," she said. There were some wooden picnic tables and benches next to the Rolling Doughnut. "I want to see the turtle," Yggdrasil said.

"You mean the fake one?" I said. "I have it here."
She looked it over.

"If the actual turtle is not igneous rock, and not sedimentary rock, and not metamorphic rock—which covers all the kinds of rock there are," Seamus Finn asked, "what does that mean? It came from outer space?"

"Obviously," Yggdrasil Birnbaum said.

"Obviously," I said.

"Obviously?" Seamus asked. "Space men brought it?"

"Or it is meteoric rock," I said.

"Ohh, a meteor!" Seamus said. "That makes sense."

"I happen to know that Steve Kraft is in his shop early on Sunday mornings," Yggdrasil said. "In fact, he lives in the back."

"So you know the place?" Seamus asked.

"I live here. I know all the places," Yggdrasil said. "We can walk over there later, and just casually take a look at the real one. I'd like to see it. Now, I think we ought to get organized. That Eucalyptus guy is going to find you, you know. He's clearly a dangerous nut— he pulled a gun on you, and he jumped out of an airplane. We ought to have some sort of plan."

"Do you think we ought to handle this ourselves?" I asked. "I mean, don't you think there should be an adult or two involved?"

"Well, my father is very much able to deal with bad men, old and weird as he is," Yggdrasil said. "And so am I, if it comes to it. What about this Sergeant Caleb you told me about? He sounds like a tough hombre."

"In addition to being Melvin the shaman, who got me involved in the first place, I am ninety-nine percent sure," I said.

"Have you confronted him and accused him of being Melvin?" Yggdrasil asked.

"No. It didn't seem polite to do so," I said.

"Oh, yes, we must be polite," Yggdrasil said. "An armed loony is sending you secret messages by television, you are in charge of some incredibly valuable doodad, and you are ninety-nine percent sure that probably the only guy who knows what's going on is working as the security guard at your school, and you're worried about being polite? Jumping horny toads! You amaze me. I don't suppose either of you knows how to handle a six-shooter. It might come to that."

Yggdrasil was wearing a plaid pinafore, with a frilly blouse and the black Mary Jane shoes with little white socks, and this time the hair ribbon was plaid. She was a girl of strange contrasts.

CHAPTER 43

A New Cadet

We got a new kid in Miss Magistra's class. Bruce Bunyip: he was big and swarthy, and had tiny eyes, a scowl, and a low forehead, and his eyebrows grew together. But his personality was not as nice as his appearance. He came into the hobby shop after school, squashed a little kid's model airplane, stuck his fist under my nose, and said, "My father is Sholmos Bunyip, the head of International Mammon Studios, and he is the richest and most powerful man in Hollywood. I have a private boxing coach, and I can, and will, if necessary, beat up every kid in this school. By the way, this watch is solid gold, and has diamonds." Then he left, probably to introduce himself to others.

"A bully and a showoff," Seamus said. "Lucky us."

"Maybe he's insecure," Al Crane said. "Thinks we're going to gang up on him, so he's trying to act tough."

"Or he's a monster, and we *should* gang up on him," I said.

"Time will tell," Seamus said. "This used to be such a peaceful military school."

"Well, if he gives me trouble, I am going to tell Iggy," I said.

Seamus and I both called Yggdrasil Iggy, but not to her face, of course. We figured she would make short work of Cadet Bruce Bunyip, and it would be interesting to see.

Al had not met Iggy yet, but naturally his father knew her father from Captain Buffalo Birnbaum's circus and Wild West show days. We were all three invited to Al's house for a hot dog supper later in the week—and since we had taken Yggdrasil into our confidence about the turtle, it didn't seem right not to tell Al, who was our friend. Al thought the story was interesting, but he may not have believed it was true. He may have thought it was just a game Seamus and I had made up. Most of the time, I didn't believe it was true myself.

Bunyip was the main topic of discussion the next

day. He had already hit a couple of people—when there was no one around to help them—and a couple of weak characters, like Stover, had become his stooges, and went around with him doing some advance threatening, and encouraging him. If he had become a bigger problem, the older cadets would have dealt with him—but he was sneaky and crafty. He knew just how far to go. He was an experienced bully. This was his third school in a year.

"I may have to straighten Cadet Bunyip out," Seamus said. "I am not my father's son for nothing."

"Is your father a tough guy?" I asked.

"Actually, no," Seamus Finn said. "But he taught me how to do the scary squint he did in *The Sword of Caravaggio*. I will dominate Bunyip with acting."

I had no confidence that this would work. The only way to dominate Bunyip would have been with a club, or maybe by taking his raw meat away. But Seamus was completely sure he could do it. He went looking for him, with Al and me trailing a safe distance behind.

Seamus found him smoking a cigarette behind the bleachers facing the parade ground. Seamus got this really serious expression, casual but with a steely look in the eyes, and sauntered up to him.

"See here, young fellow," Seamus Finn said to the

mouth-breathing bully. "You're new, and obviously don't know how to behave, so I'm going to give you the benefit of the doubt and assume that you're a good chap and want to fit in. Isn't that so?"

"Yes, sir," Bunyip said. It was working! Al and I couldn't believe it.

"Let's have no more slugging people, and you'll get along fine," Seamus said. "If I hear any more bad reports about you . . . well, we have a tradition of dueling here, and I am captain of the junior saber team. If you look closely, you'll see that a couple of the cadets have an artificial ear. I think you understand." While he said this he looked exactly like Count Caravaggio, the greatest swordsman in Italy.

"I can get you a pass to visit the movie studio," Bunyip said.

Seamus did this excellent chuckle. "My father is Aaron Finn," he said. "I visit the studio whenever I like."

"Ohh," Bruce Bunyip said. He stuck his hand out. "I hope we can be friends."

Seamus shook his hand. "We'll see. No more playful punches, agreed?" Bunyip nodded. He looked grateful.

"Now off with you, you rascal," Seamus said. And Bunyip lurched off harmlessly.

"That was incredible!" Al said.

"How did you do it?" I asked Seamus.

"I watch my father practicing," Seamus said. "He says anybody can be an actor. Bunyip is still an idiot, but he may keep his hands to himself now."

Another interesting thing happened that day. As Seamus and I were passing the main gate, Sergeant Caleb called us over. "Tighten your necktie, Wentworthstein," he said. "And, yes, I am Melvin."

"You admit it?" I asked.

"Your friend Yggdrasil stopped by this morning," Sergeant Caleb said. "Did you know she is the daughter of Captain Buffalo Birnbaum? A man of great honor among the Indian people."

"So are you going to explain everything about the turtle?" I asked Sergeant Melvin the shaman Caleb.

"In due course. I will tell you everything, but not now. I have to direct traffic, and holler at the cadets. Good afternoon, gentlemen."

CHAPTER 44

Hot Dog Supper

The Faceless Man called Yggdrasil Iggy and she did not pop him in the nose—how could she? Besides the fact that he had no nose to pop, he was so friendly and informal, like all the circus people, that Yggdrasil would have seemed stuck up and stuffy if she had corrected him. Al Crane called her Iggy too, and soon everyone did, Seamus and me included. She was stuck with it—and it didn't seem to bother her. In fact, she was having a good time at the hot dog supper at the Cranes'. She must have known that Seamus and I were going to call her Iggy from then on. Yggdrasil is the name of the tree that connects heaven, earth, and hell in Norse mythology, and it is a weird name for a person.

The Faceless Man, whose name was Peter, was

one of the sideshow freaks with the Gibbs Brothers
Circus. He kept his mask on while we ate—the top
part was a Lone Ranger type of mask, and the rest was
like a little curtain or veil that covered his face . . .
well, his nonface. He sort of worked the food up under the edge of the veil, while conversing in a very
amusing fashion. It turned out he spoke five languages
and had degrees from three universities in Europe.

The other guest, besides us kids, was Clive Montague himself, the main attraction and wild animal
tamer with the circus. He was a little guy with quick,
dark eyes and really nice clothes. He had been all over
the world capturing wild animals, and he had lots of
good stories.

The meal, as promised, was all hot dogs. Al's
mother served them Texas-style with chili, New
York—style with mustard and sauerkraut, and
Chicago-style with mustard, green pickle relish,
chopped onions, tomato slices, hot peppers, and cel-
ery salt. Also, she tucked a kosher pickle spear into
each bun. The only guest who could eat one of these
without making a mess was Peter the Faceless Man.
Clive Montague had to tie a napkin around his neck
like a bib. The grownups drank beer, and there was
root beer for the kids. It was the best dinner party I
had ever been to.

All the grownups had good stories to tell about life in the circus, and animals they had known, and in Peter's case, about hanging out with Professor Einstein in Switzerland. Einstein, the smartest guy in the world—they were still friends, and Einstein always got a free ticket when the circus played Princeton, New Jersey. Peter said he had helped Einstein do some calculations based on the performance of the aerialists—those are the high trapeze artists—and showed them how to improve their act.

Clive Montague told about catching full-grown tigers in Sumatra, and living with the native people, and how two pythons put the squeeze on him at the same time.

Al's father told about the time Sadie, my favorite elephant, had gotten loose and wandered away north of Poughkeepsie, New York, and spent a whole day on her own, turning up in people's backyards and stopping traffic.

And Al's mother played the banjo, and the Faceless Man sang Russian songs. He had a beautiful voice. Then we heard something between a meow and a blood-chilling scream.

"Ah, the leopards are awake," Clive Montague said. "They'll be wanting their bottles." He went to one of the bedrooms and brought out a carton with two baby black leopards in it. "Too young to be left alone," Clive Montague said. "So I brought them along."

These animals were so beautiful, they made us whisper. They were blackest black, with regular leopard spots in an even blacker blackest black. Clive Montague let us play with them and give them their bottles.

"*Melanistic* is what you call it when they come black like this," he said. "They can be born to regular spotted leopards, and with a spotted littermate or two. These little chaps will get to be as much as two hundred pounds, and you'll never guess where they come from."

"Africa?" Iggy said.

"India?" I said.

"Siberia?" Seamus said.

"I know where, so I won't guess," Al Crane said.

"They come from the wilds of Scotland," Clive Montague said.

"Scotland? So they were bred in captivity?" Iggy asked.

"They are wild-born," Clive Montague said. "Not many people know there are still leopards in the British Isles. They're incredibly hard to find, clever as they are. They live wild in this country too, in places like Ohio and Michigan. They're man-eaters as well. Usually a pet will disappear, or the family cow, and no one will know what happened—but sometimes it's Uncle Fred. It's leopards more times than you'd think."

I had a little man-eater in my lap, sucking away at a baby bottle and looking very content.

"These little chaps are with me all the time," Clive Montague said. "They have a future as circus stars, and they won't eat me, because I'm their mommy."

"Mr. Montague, what do you know about sacred turtles?" Iggy asked.

CHAPTER 45

Too Horrible to Tell

"Sacred turtles?" Clive Montague said. "Let me see . . . there's the Giant Turtle of Sumatra, but that is a story too horrible to tell. Then there is the Turtle Temple of Colombo, Ceylon. The monks there nurse sick and injured turtles back to health and return them to the wild. There's the Kwakiutl turtle dance— takes hours and hours—and the Jivaro Turtle Society. There's the great turtle statue in Kamakura, the singing turtles of the Amazon, the early and completely unsuccessful submarine of Peruvian design called 'the Turtle,' and Leo the Turtle, the trademark and mascot of International Mammon Studios—you must have seen it at the beginning of every picture. Sholmos Bunyip, the owner of the studio, is a great collector of turtle art. He has turtles made of wood, marble, malachite, alabaster, gold, halvah, and every precious substance—also paintings, mosaics, frescoes, tapestries, all of turtles. But I don't think I have ever heard of a sacred turtle as such."

"There are stories of a sacred turtle," Peter the Faceless Man broke in. "It is made of meteoric stone, quite small in size. The Native American peoples consider it to have remarkable magical powers, though it is not certain it is of Indian origin. It may be the turtle written about by Herodotus and Xenophon in the fifth century B.C. Ptolemy the Fifth of Egypt is said to have had such a turtle around 192 B.C. Constantine the Great may have had it in the fourth century A.D. It somehow found its way to Vienna in the eighteenth century. The story goes that Lorenzo Da Ponte got the turtle from Casanova, and had it with him when he arrived in Philadelphia in 1805. When Da Ponte died in 1838, he left the turtle in his will to an American Indian friend of his, Mad Rabbit, of the wolf clan of the Tuscarora nation of the six-nation Iroquois confederacy. After that, the turtle was in Native American hands, and ultimately all record of it was lost. Of course, I don't know if any of this is true. It's a story I was told by an old man in an all-night doughnut shop in Jersey City years and years ago."

"Did the old man say what was so magic, or so sacred, about the turtle?" Iggy asked.

"No, he did not," Peter the Faceless Man said. "And now that I think of it, he seemed to be quite mad. It is, if it really exists, the rarest and most valuable turtle, real or artificial, on the planet."

"Sounds like it," Clive Montague said. "Sholmos Bunyip would probably pay millions for a turtle like that. I say, Peter, let's have another Russian song!"

CHAPTER 46

On the Way Home

Walking back to the Hermione Hotel after our hot dog supper at Al's house, Yggdrasil said, "Those baby leopards were cute."

"Yes, they were, Iggy," I said. Iggy smiled, and did not pop me in the nose.

"That was some story Peter the Faceless Man told about the turtle," Seamus said. "Do you think it could be as old as that?"

"He said it *may* be the turtle that was written about by Herodotus, and those other guys," Iggy said. "It may be. It could just be a story."

"Or it could be true," Seamus said.

"I want to have another look at it," Iggy said. "Let's drop in at Stuffed Stuff 'n' Stuff tomorrow."

"What I don't understand is why Melvin the shaman gave it to me in the first place," I said. "If it's so old and valuable, I mean."

"We should ask him," Seamus said. "Sergeant Caleb admitted he was Melvin the shaman. And, by the way, how could he be in Albuquerque, New Mexico, just when you happened to come through, when he's at the school every day?"

"Yes, we need to ask him about that too," I said.

"You don't suppose he gave the turtle to Neddie in order to smuggle it to California?" Iggy said. "Maybe so he could sell it to that turtle-collecting guy, Sholmos Bunyip?"

"The father of the idiot Bunyip who goes to our school," Seamus said.

"No, I don't think Melvin is like that," I said.

"I don't either," Seamus Finn said. "Sergeant Caleb wouldn't do anything sneaky."

"Besides, why would he give me the turtle to smuggle for him, and then tell everybody? Half the people I met on the way here knew about it. Of course, a couple of them were him."

We walked some more.

"I want to work in the circus, and maybe go on wild animal–collecting expeditions, like Clive Montague," Iggy said.

"So do I," Seamus said.

"I do too," I said.

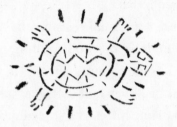

CHAPTER 47

Gone!

The next day was Sunday, and Seamus and I were going to miss waffles again to have breakfast with Iggy. We had tried to get her to have breakfast at our apartment, but she wanted to go to the Rolling Doughnut again. She said it was traditional.

When Iggy turned up in the lobby of the Hermione Hotel, she was wearing blue jeans instead of her usual frilly dress! She also had on a gray sweatshirt, the kind with a hood attached, and basketball shoes. Seamus and I were amazed.

"I didn't think you even owned clothes like that," Seamus said.

"If I am going to be called Iggy, I may as well look

like an Iggy," Iggy said. "You will miss the woman of elegance I used to be."

Iggy, in her informal costume, fit in better with the slob clientele at the Rolling Doughnut. We had coffee with our doughnuts again—it was the only place Seamus or I ever had coffee. Whether kids are supposed to drink coffee is a sort of gray area. Some people think it's bad for kids and will lead them to cigarettes or maybe juvenile delinquency. Some don't think it matters. Seamus and I put lots and lots of milk and sugar in ours. Iggy had hers black.

After three doughnuts and two coffees apiece, we strolled over to Stuffed Stuff 'n' Stuff. The door was unlocked as always, and Steve Kraft was having breakfast.

"Care for doughnuts, kids?" Steve said. "I'm afraid all I have to drink is coffee—I don't suppose you use it."

"We've had our breakfast, thanks," Iggy said. "Mind if we just browse around?"

"Go ahead. Educate yourselves," Steve said. "If you want to know about anything, just holler."

We threaded through the narrow aisles between the stuffed animals, the fake works of art, and the spooky made-up medical specimens in jars. When we got to the place where Steve kept his fake sacred turtle—really the real sacred turtle—it wasn't there! We were only a little worried—probably Steve Kraft had moved it. We looked around but didn't see it.

"Steve," Seamus said, "where did you put the sacred turtle that was here next to the stuffed jack-a-lope?"

"Gone," Steve said, with a mouth full of doughnut.

"Gone? You sold it? You told us you would never sell it!"

"I hadn't planned to," Steve Kraft said. "It was my finest work of fakery. But this guy came in and made me such an offer! I just had to let it go."

"You sold it? You sold it?"

"I'm going to make another, and he not only gave me a huge wad of money—he threw in an almost authentic Eskimo hunting hat. You just can't get those—even phony ones. Want to see it?"

"You sold the turtle? You said you would never sell the turtle!"

"Well, it's a store. People buy things. He paid me a thousand dollars. Guy must have been nuts."

"Who was this guy?" Iggy asked.

"It was Nick Bluegum. A well-known collector.

By the way, he really does have blue gums," Steve said.

"Nick Bluegum!" Seamus whispered.

"Also known as Sandor Eucalyptus!" I whispered.

"Oh, this is bad, isn't it?" Iggy whispered.

"I think it's very bad," I said.

CHAPTER 48

Very Bad

There was only one thing to do. We found a pay phone, and I dialed the number of the main gate at Brown-Sparrow. Sergeant Caleb—Melvin the shaman—answered.

"Sergeant . . . Melvin . . . it's Neddie. We need to talk to you. It's serious."

"I bet it's something about the turtle," Sergeant Melvin said. "I'm just going off duty. You know where the Rolling Doughnut is? I'll meet you there in twenty minutes."

CHAPTER 49

Questions and Answers

When Sergeant Caleb turned up at the Rolling Doughnut, he was not wearing his crisp marine uniform. He was not wearing the plain nondescript clothes he wore when I met him as Melvin the shaman. He was wearing a red and black striped sweater, black and white shoes, and a little black cap with a red pompom on top—also big sunglasses with black plastic frames. He got four jelly doughnuts, and four coffees, and carried them to the picnic table where Seamus, Iggy, and I were sitting, waiting for him.

"I got Bismarcks for everyone," Sergeant Caleb said.

"Bismarcks?"

"Named for Otto von Bismarck, born 1815, died 1898, prime minister of Prussia from 1862 to 1873, and the chancellor of Germany from 1871 to 1890. I don't know what he had to do with jelly doughnuts—maybe he liked them."

Before this, we had ordered plain doughnuts at the Rolling Doughnut. We bit into the Bismarcks and they squirted jelly, into our mouths and down our chins. They were all right, but I didn't think I would be switching to them on future visits.

"Archaeologists have found petrified doughnuts in prehistoric ruins in the Southwest," Sergeant Caleb said. "No one knows how far back they go. The Dutch made *olie-koecken*, or oily-cakes—the Puritans ate them. Some people credit the modern doughnut to the mother of Captain Hanson Crockett Gregory, a sea captain—his mother used to make them for him to take on his voyages. Captain Gregory claimed to be the first person to knock a hole in the middle of an oily-cake."

"That's very interesting," I said. "But we wanted to talk about—"

"There's more," Sergeant Caleb said. "In the 1920s, a Russian immigrant living in New York, named Adolph Levitt, invented a doughnut machine—probably just like the one here at the Rolling Doughnut.

Machine-made doughnuts were a sensation at the Chicago World's Fair of 1934, and Levitt made millions selling doughnut machines."

"Are you actually a real shaman?" I asked Sergeant Caleb.

"I am a retired sergeant in the United States Marine Corps," Sergeant Caleb said. "And a shaman, but I don't practice."

"Are you really a Navajo Indian?" I asked, quickly, before he could shift back to the history of doughnuts.

"Everybody who knows me says I am," Sergeant Caleb said. "You can ask anyone."

This was sort of a twisty answer—but to press the question would have been impolite, as if I were accusing him of posing as a Navajo. I decided he wasn't, but I didn't know what that might mean one way or the other.

Seamus Finn abandoned specific questions and tried another approach. "Tell us everything about the turtle."

"It's very old," Sergeant Melvin Caleb said. "No one knows for sure how old." He took a sip of his coffee. Then he sat there silently. He was good at silences.

Back to direct questions, I asked, "Does it have special powers? Magical ones?"

"Yes." Melvin was ready to tell us the whole history of the common doughnut, but getting him to talk about what *we* wanted him to talk about was a heavy struggle.

"Where did you get it?" Iggy asked.

"I got it from another shaman," Melvin said.

"Another shaman?" Iggy followed up.

"Yes."

"What was his name?" Iggy wasn't going to quit.

"Ed."

"Ed? His name was Ed?" Iggy sounded calm, but she was tapping her basketball shoe under the table.

"Yes. Ed the shaman."

"Do I have to ask where Ed the shaman got it?"

"From another shaman. I think her name was Susie."

"So, are we correct in assuming the turtle has gone from shaman to shaman for a long time?" Iggy asked.

"That's right," Melvin said.

"And why did you give the turtle to Neddie?" Iggy asked. "He's not a shaman."

"You don't know that he's not," Melvin said.

"I'm not," I said.

"You don't know that you're not," Melvin said. "People are shamans before they know they are—so you could be. And the reason I gave the turtle to Neddie was that I was told to."

"Who told you to, another shaman?" Seamus asked.

"Maybe. Maybe it was another shaman. Maybe it was a whole lot of shamans. Most likely it was the turtle itself. Anyway, I knew I was supposed to give it to him."

"The turtle itself told you to give it to me?"

"More or less."

"Do you know why you were supposed to give it to me?"

"You realize this is official shaman stuff we're talking about, and technically I'm not supposed to discuss it with anybody," Melvin said. "But to answer your question, not exactly. I suppose because you were the next step in the turtle's destiny—but I'm only guessing."

Iggy was waving her hand in the air as though she were in class. "Oooh! Oooh! What is the turtle's destiny?"

"Every so often . . . not very often, really . . . every hundred years, or several hundred years, there's a kind of . . . thing that happens."

"Thing? What kind of thing?"

"Well, like an eruption, or an earthquake, but not

exactly. It's not just like this, but it's sort of as if there were very old powers, underground, sort of, and they are dead, only they aren't. Once in a while they wake up and try to come back, and if that were to happen everything would go topsy-turvy. Imagine if all of a sudden there were dinosaurs again, or saber-tooth cats, things like that."

"I might like to see that," Iggy said.

"Not close up, you wouldn't," Melvin said. "Anyway, the turtle plays a role when that happens— it helps keep things from getting out of order. Sort of stabilizes things—up is up, down is down, alive is alive, and extinct is extinct. Turtle is very important. Sort of an evolutionary compass."

"Uh-oh," I said.

CHAPTER 50

A Serious Mistake

"Um, Sergeant Caleb, I sort of lost the turtle," I said.

"Lost it?"

Then I told Sergeant Caleb all about switching the turtle with the fake turtle at Steve Kraft's store, and how I thought it would be safe if Sandor Eucalyptus, also known as Nick Bluegum, caught up with me, but he caught up with the turtle instead, and how I knew that he, Melvin the shaman, had told me to take care of it, and how I was very sorry and had made a serious mistake.

"Anybody want another doughnut?" Melvin asked. "I'm going to have one."

"Wait!" I said. "It's pretty serious that I let the turtle fall into that guy's hands, isn't it?"

"I don't know," Sergeant Melvin said. "Maybe that is the turtle's destiny. Maybe you were supposed to do that. Maybe it told you to do that."

"We have an idea that Nick Bluegum is going to sell the turtle to a guy named Sholmos Bunyip," Iggy said. "He's raving mad for turtles and really rich."

"Well, if that happens, it's probably what's supposed to happen," Sergeant Shaman said. "I don't suppose there would be any harm unless Sholmos Bunyip is an evil person. Then it might be serious."

"We know his son," Seamus said.

"Is he an evil person?" the sergeant asked.

"He shows every sign of being one," Seamus said.

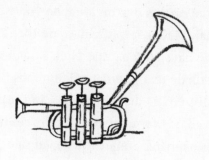

CHAPTER 51

What to Do?

"What should we do?" I asked Sergeant Caleb.

"Do about what?" Sergeant Caleb asked.

"About the turtle," I said.

"You think there's something we should be do-ing?"

"Yes. What if Sholmos Bunyip is an evil person? What if the turtle falls into his hands? What if one of those events, like the old powers waking up, happens?"

"First of all, those events . . . that's a good word for it, *events* . . . happen a long time apart. When the next one happens, Sholmos Bunyip might be long gone and the turtle might have moved on many times. Anyway, it's your turtle—for now—I gave it to you. No one gave it to Nick Bluegum, and if he sells it, no one will have given it to whomever he sells it to. A thing like that has to be given—it can't be sold, traded, or stolen. You have to give it to the next person, and something will tell you when it's time to do that, and whom to give it to."

"But I don't even have it," I said.

"You have the one you switched at that fellow's store," Sergeant Caleb said.

"Yes, but it's a fake," I said.

"Is it? Let's see it," Melvin the shaman said. I dug the turtle out of my pocket and handed it to Sergeant Caleb.

"Pretty good," he said. "I tell you what . . . hang on to this one, and don't worry about anything."

I was confused.

"I hope you boys realize that, even though we've had doughnuts together, when we meet at school, conduct must be strictly military," Sergeant Caleb said.

"Yes, Sergeant Caleb," Seamus and I said.

"No 'How's it going, Melvin?' or anything like that, especially if anyone else is around."

We understood.

"Well, I'm going to the music store now to see if they have a new Dizzy Gillespie record. Don't worry, Cadet Wentworthstein. Everything is in good order."

"Thanks for the Bismarcks," we said.

CHAPTER 52

Doctor Seamus

Bruce Bunyip was showing signs of becoming antisocial again. I should say more antisocial—he had continued to be repellent and obnoxious, but had backed off of slugging people after Seamus Finn crushed him in a contest of wills. Now, after having time to get used to the school, and also to sprout a monster wart on his sloping forehead, he was starting to threaten again.

"I think Cadet Bunyip needs another session," Seamus Finn said.

"Are you going to do Count Caravaggio again?" Al asked him.

"No, this time I am going to do Dr. Hershberg, the

kindly psychiatrist, as played by my father in *Ode to Freud,* a change-of-pace role."

Seamus somehow made his face soft and his eyes sad and friendly. We followed him, looking for Bunyip. We found him behind the gym, stripping the bark off a tree.

Seamus put his hand on Bunyip's burly shoulder. "You're not a happy boy, are you, Bruce?" Seamus said softly.

"I'm not?" the abominable Bunyip asked.

"People don't appreciate you," Seamus said.

"They don't!" Bunyip said.

"You're sensitive."

"I am!" Bunyip said. "I have a kitten at home, and I don't torture it or anything."

"Of course you don't," Seamus said. "You love your kitten."

"My mommy doesn't love me!" Bunyip wailed. "She went back to Switzerland. She says my father is a monster and I'm a monster too."

"How sad," Seamus said.

"I hate the Swiss," Bunyip said.

"Everybody does."

"If I peel the bark off all the way around, this tree will die."

"You hate the tree," Seamus said, stroking Bunyip's greasy hair.

"Yes, I hate the tree," Bunyip said, sniffling.

"Of course you do. Why do you hate the tree, Bruce?"

"Because it's Swiss?"

"It's a Swiss tree?"

"I dunno."

"Will you be happy if the tree dies?" Seamus asked.

"I guess so. My father *is* a monster. He yells and screams, and everybody is afraid of him."

"Are you afraid of him?" Seamus asked.

Bunyip wiped his nose. "Sometimes he smiles—that's really scary. When he is nice to people at the studio, sometimes they faint. Usually when he looks happy it's because he is going to do something horrible to someone."

"You like to do horrible things to people," Seamus said.

"Well, yes," Bunyip said.

"Why is that, Bruce? Why do you like to do horrible things to people?"

"I don't know. 'Cause I'm good at it?"

"Is it because, when you do horrible things to

them, then they know how you feel when your father smiles at you?"

"My brain hurts," Bunyip said.

"I tell you what," Seamus said. "Let's let this tree live."

"You think?" Bunyip asked.

"I do. Leave the tree alone. And maybe don't start in bashing other cadets. Can you do that for me, Bruce?"

"I'll try," Bunyip said.

"I think you should go into the gym and shoot some baskets," Seamus said.

"I like to shoot baskets," Bunyip said.

"Good boy. I'm proud of you."

Bunyip loped off into the gym to shoot baskets.

"That was magnificent," I said.

"If he weren't so dangerous, I'd feel sorry for him," Al said.

"That will hold him for a while," Seamus said. "It seems the thing to do is get him thinking. Since he can't do two things at once, he's unlikely to throw punches when his brain, such as it is, is active."

"You were great," I said. "And you got this from copying your father's role as a psychiatrist? What picture was that again?"

"It's a stinker. He plays a psychiatrist who is also the greatest swordsman in Vienna."

"Bunyip's father sounds pretty horrible," Al said.

"Oh, he is," Seamus said. "My father has told me stories about him. You know the woman who works at the Rolling Doughnut?"

"The real pretty one who talks to herself and drools?" I asked.

"That's the one. She was all set to be a big movie star, like Betty Grable or somebody. Had already made two pictures, and they were going to release them with all kinds of publicity and make sure she was a big success."

"So what happened?" Al asked.

"Sholmos Bunyip got mad at her for some reason—or no reason. He threw out the pictures, made it so nobody would give her a job—not just in movies—she couldn't get any job anywhere in Los Angeles. For a while she was sleeping on those benches at bus stops and wearing newspapers."

"That's really harsh," I said.

"Every few weeks, Bunyip comes by and orders a doughnut and laughs at her," Seamus said. "He's a monster, all right."

And he probably has my turtle by now, I thought.

CHAPTER 53

A Normal Saturday

Seamus, Al, Iggy, and I were crowded into one of the little booths at the big music store on Sunset and Vine. We were listening to "Night in Tunisia" by Dizzy Gillespie. The way it worked was like this: There was a row of little rooms along one side of the store, with windows onto the street, glass doors, and windows into the store. There was a turntable in each booth, and you could take records into one and listen to them to see if you wanted to buy them. The trick was to act in a way to convince the clerks that you were really going to buy a record and weren't just listening for free. The clerks were young guys, and nobody ever saw them kick anybody out for playing a lot of records and not buying any—but we put on an act just the same. When we brought records back from the booth, we said things like, "I am seriously considering purchasing this recording—but I would prefer to think about it for a while. Very probably, I will come back tomorrow, or possibly even later today, and buy it—perhaps several copies, to give as gifts to my friends and family."

The clerks would look bored, and say, "Fine. You want to listen to anything else?"

You could get kicked out of the music store for dancing, eating, or sleeping in the listening booths, but we never did those things.

So there we were, all jammed into the booth, listening to "Night in Tunisia." We wanted to hear what Dizzy Gillespie sounded like, because Sergeant Caleb had mentioned him. He was pretty amazing.

Through the glass door of the booth, we all noticed a guy wearing a fur hat with what looked like buffalo horns coming out of the sides. He had long hair braided into two pigtails, and was wearing a suit and tie. He was browsing in the classical music section. Nobody mentioned him—we were too involved with following Dizzy's music—but we all saw him.

The record ended, and we had breathed up most of the air in the booth, so we went outside and wandered east along Sunset Boulevard. We hadn't gone very far when a teenager in an NBC uniform approached us.

"Would you like free tickets to a radio broadcast?" the teenager asked politely. He was an NBC page—it's a job kids can get. We accepted the tickets. "Show begins in ten minutes," the page said. "Right through that door."

This was something the others had done lots of times but that I hadn't yet—being in the audience at radio shows. The programs needed people to laugh and applaud, and sometimes participate in games and quizzes. It was free, and we were just kicking around the streets on a Saturday afternoon, following a morning at the Hitching Post. Seamus and Al and I did things like this every Saturday. Iggy went to the Harmonious Reality School, a progressive school down the street, and could just walk out whenever she felt like it. Sometimes she would sit in the audience at a weekday program, and read or take a nap. She said her school was not to be taken seriously.

CHAPTER 54

Live Audience

It was like a little theater, like a movie house, with nice seats, and a stage with microphones where the screen would be. About half the seats had people in them. We sat in the last row, so we could sneak out if it was boring.

A guy in a suit came out. "Welcome to the radio broadcast of *Who Knows?* This is what we call the audience warm-up. *Who Knows?* is a quiz program. We're going to select contestants from among the audience, so when we ask who wants to play, raise your hand if you do—and if one of the NBC pages points to you, come directly down to the stage. In a few minutes we're going to begin the game. We hope you'll enjoy our show, and please show your appreciation when the sign that says 'Applause' lights up.

"Now, this is very important: when the sign that says 'Who Knows?' lights up, and I point to the audience, I want you all to shout, 'Who knows?' nice and loud. Let's give it a try, okay?"

The "Who Knows?" sign lit up, and the guy in the suit pointed, and we all hollered, "Who knows?"

"That was great," the guy in the suit said. "And now let's welcome our quizmaster, Ed Eft! Give him a big hand, folks!"

The applause sign lit up and Ed Eft came out. We whistled and clapped. Behind a glass window, there were guys with earphones on pointing and signaling to Ed.

"Welcome, welcome to *Who Knows?*" Ed Eft said, "the quiz program where ordinary people can win up to one hundred dollars. Who is going to have a chance to play our game, and possibly win big money?"

The sign lit up, the guy in the suit pointed, and we all shouted, "Who knows?"

"Now, let's see who is going to play with us today," Ed Eft said. "Raise your hands, members of the audience, if you want to play. Raise them nice and high." We all raised our hands.

"When the NBC page points to you, come right down to the stage. Ohhh, look at all the hands! Okay, the gentleman with horns on his hat—hurry on down, sir! And the little girl in the back row! Come on down and play *Who Knows?*"

It was the guy we had seen in the music store, and the other contestant was going to be Iggy!

"Wow! Iggy is going to be on the radio!" Seamus said.

"And look!" Al said. "The other contestant is the weirdball with the horny hat we saw in the record store!"

Iggy and the weirdball were on the stage with Ed Eft.

"And who do we have here?" Ed Eft said. "What is your name, sir?"

"I am Nishdugedak," the guy with the horns said. "You may address me as Crazy Wig."

"You are a Native American, I presume," Ed Eft said.

"I am Crazy Wig."

"Can I call you Chief Crazy Wig?"

"No."

"And what is your name, sweet little girl?"

"I am Yggdrasil Birnbaum," Iggy said. "You may address me as Iggy."

"Do you know how we play our game?" Ed Eft said.

"No idea," Crazy Wig said.

"No idea," Iggy said.

"You may choose from one of our categories," Ed Eft said. "I will ask you ten questions. Each question is worth five dollars. If you give a wrong answer we deduct five dollars. And if you answer all the questions correctly, you will divide a hundred dollars between you. Can they do it, audience?"

The light came on and the guy in the suit pointed. We all shouted, "Who knows?"

"Here are the categories," Ed Eft said. "Cowboy Stars of the Silver Screen . . . "

"Pick that one, Iggy," we whispered.

"Her father is a cowboy star of the silver screen," I whispered to Al. "She probably knows all about it."

"The next category is Indian Legends and Lore."

"Pick that one," we whispered, thinking that Crazy Wig, a Native American, would know all about it.

"And the third category is Turtles."

"Turtles," Iggy said.

"Turtles," Crazy Wig said.

"Turtles?" we whispered.

CHAPTER 55

Turtles?

"The category you've chosen is Turtles, and here is the first question. How many kinds of turtles are there?"

Iggy and Crazy Wig whispered to each other.

"Shot down," Al said.

"How can they possibly know that?" Seamus asked.

"We're going to say two hundred seventy, Ed," Crazy Wig said.

"And the answer is," Ed said, "two hundred seventy! You're off to a good start, contestants! You have five dollars. Answer the next question correctly and get another five dollars—but remember, a wrong answer will cost you five dollars! Now, for another five dollars, how long have turtles been on earth?"

They didn't even whisper this time.

"Turtles have been here since before the dinosaurs," Iggy said.

"It's about two hundred and thirty million years, Ed," Crazy Wig said.

"That's right! Chief Crazy Wig and little Iggy Birnbaum, you have ten dollars! But there's another question coming. Will they get it right, audience?"

"Who knows?"

"This is a tough one," Ed Eft said. "Can turtles hear, and do they have ears?"

"Turtles don't have an outer ear, Ed," Crazy Wig said.

"But they do have an inner ear, and can hear," Iggy said.

"Answer this next one, and you'll have twenty dollars," Ed Eft said. "What is the largest turtle?"

"It's the leatherback sea turtle at ninety-five inches long, Ed," Crazy Wig said.

"The largest tortoise is the Galápagos tortoise," Iggy said, "and the largest freshwater turtle in the United States is the alligator snapping turtle."

"You anticipate our next question, little Yggdrasil," Ed Eft said. "Is there a difference between a tortoise and a turtle?"

"There is, Ed," Iggy said. "In North America we

call them tortoises if they live on land, and turtles if they need constant access to water. And there is one type of turtle we call a terrapin—it's the diamond-back terrapin, and it lives in brackish, or slightly salty, water."

"But in Europe, only sea turtles are referred to as turtles," Crazy Wig said. "Freshwater varieties are called terrapins, and land-based varieties are called tortoises, including box turtles, which need access to water."

"Twenty-five dollars, and not a single wrong answer!" Ed Eft said. "Get five more right, and divide a hundred dollars between you. Now, here's a toughie—what do turtles do in the winter?"

"They brummate, Ed."

"Correct! They brummate, which is another word for hibernate. You're doing great, contestants. And we'll be right back to play this exciting game, after a word from Mad Man Muntz, maker of Muntz television sets."

The guy in the suit read an advertisement for television sets, and said the name of the radio station, and what time it was.

Seamus and Al and I were pretty excited. Between them, Crazy Wig and Iggy appeared to know all there was to know about turtles. After the commercial, the questions and answers resumed.

Smallest turtle? The bog turtle, or Muhlenberg's turtle. Smallest tortoise? The speckled cape padloper. Can turtles take off their shells? No.

"And now for our last question," Ed Eft said. "Get this one right, and divide a hundred dollars. What is meant by Turtle Island?"

"I'll take this one," Crazy Wig said. "This is . . . this North American continent is Turtle Island, and the reason is that, according to Amerindian belief, this land is supported on the back of a great turtle."

"That is absolutely correct!" Ed Eft shouted. "A perfect score, and our contestants, Chief Crazy Wig and Yggdrasil Birnbaum, win one hundred dollars!"

The applause sign was flashing on and off, and we were stamping and clapping and cheering and whistling.

"I'd like to say something, Ed," Crazy Wig said.

"Certainly, Chief," Ed Eft said.

"Los Angeles is in great peril, maybe doomed," Crazy Wig said. "Ancient prophesies tell us that a huge catastrophe is about to happen. Gigantic animals nobody has ever seen before will be rampaging in the streets. People won't know which way to run. I am going to spend my fifty dollars on a bus ticket out of here, and I advise everyone else to do the same."

"Chief Crazy Wig, ladies and gentlemen!" Ed Eft said, clapping his hands. "A great contestant! Let's give the chief a big round of applause!"

Yaaay! Clap, clap, clap, clap, clap.

CHAPTER 56

They're Back!

Al had to go. His family was invited to a birthday party for the bearded lady from the circus. Seamus, Iggy, and I headed back toward the Hermione. We saw Crazy Wig having an Orange Julius at the stand on Vine Street. "Nice working with you, partner," he said to Iggy.

"That stuff you said . . . about the catastrophe . . ." I said.

"I said something about a catastrophe?" Crazy Wig said. "I wonder what it was."

"You don't remember?"

"Sometimes I don't pay attention. I may have been tired and confused after remembering all that stuff about turtles. Well, it was fun winning money with you, Yggdrasil. I have to go now—have a bus to catch."

Crazy Wig headed off toward the bus station.

"So is he a loony or what?" I asked.

"He knows plenty about turtles," Seamus said.

"Hey, I answered some of those questions," Iggy said.

When we got back to the Hermione, who should be sitting in the lobby but Aaron Finn—and Billy the Phantom Bellboy!

"Father!" Seamus said.

"Son!" Aaron said.

"Neddie!" Billy said.

"Ghost!" I said.

"This is Yggdrasil Birnbaum," Seamus said.

"Call me Iggy," Iggy said. "I've gotten used to it."

"Not the daughter of Captain Buffalo Birnbaum!" Aaron Finn said. "I was at your birthday party when you were one year old! How is your dear father?"

"The same as always," Iggy said. "He and my mother live right here in the hotel."

"I must look him up soon," Aaron Finn said. "What a fine gentleman he is. And Neddie, we saw your parents. They're picking up your sister at a play rehearsal, and then we're going to meet them at the

Brown Derby, if you have no other plans. And of course Yggdrasil is welcome to come too, if she likes."

"My sister is in a play?" I asked.

"They're doing *A Streetcar Named West Pico Boulevard* at the high school," Aaron Finn said.

"How was Canada?" Seamus asked his father.

"It went well," Aaron Finn said. "I had a good role—I played a Mountie who is the greatest swordsman in Saskatchewan. And while I was there, I wrote my own screenplay, with Billy's help."

"Actually, I did most of the writing," Billy said. "But we're going to put your father's name on it."

"So, you're a ghostwriter?" Iggy said.

"Very funny," Billy said. "It's about a vampire who is the greatest swordsman in Transylvania, and becomes a pirate. We're calling it *Captain Bloodthirsty*."

"We can shoot the whole thing in the IMS tank," Aaron Finn said.

International Mammon Studios has this huge tank, like a gigantic swimming pool. I could see a corner of it in the distance from one of my bedporch windows. It was big enough to put ships in, and had a great big billboard behind it painted to look like the sky. Just as big was the full-size stucco replica of the Roman Coliseum they'd been building for weeks.

"We brought your parents a forty-seven-pound Canadian cheese," Aaron Finn said. "And look, boys! We brought you each a Mountie hat."

"Neat!" Seamus and I said, and tried on the hats.

Aaron Finn lowered his voice. "Does your friend know about the item?"

"The item?"

"The gadget, the thing, the shtick, the gimmick, the whatzit . . . You know, the thing . . . that Neddie has . . . the little stone thing."

"Oh, the turtle! Yes, Iggy is our friend. She knows all about it—and we have things to tell you."

"We have things to tell you too," Aaron Finn said. "We ran into Melvin the shaman in Canada."

"What?"

"You know, the shaman—the one who gave Neddie the turtle."

"How is that possible? He's working at Brown-Sparrow! We see him every day!"

"That Melvin!" Billy said. "He's full of tricks, isn't he?"

So we sat there in the lobby of the Hermione Hotel, Seamus and me wearing our Mountie hats, and told Aaron Finn and Billy the Phantom Bellboy all the things that had happened, about Nick Bluegum being Sandor Eucalyptus and sending me a secret message, and how Sergeant Caleb was Melvin, and how I had hidden the turtle at Stuffed Stuff 'n' Stuff, how Steve Kraft had sold it to Nick Bluegum, and our belief that Bluegum would sell it to Sholmos Bunyip—right up to the quiz show and Crazy Wig.

"I know Crazy Wig," Billy said. "He is well named."

"You know everybody," I said to Billy.

"You haunt a hotel for forty-three years, and you meet them all," he said.

CHAPTER 57

Fat Cat in the Hat

"How many Melvin the shamans do you suppose there are?" I asked. We were in Aaron Finn's Packard, heading for the Brown Derby.

"Just the one," Billy the Phantom Bellboy said.

"Then how can he be in two or more places at the same time?"

"Don't try to figure it out. It will just make you dizzy," Billy said. "Shamans can do stuff. You know how people always say there's a reasonable explanation for things like this? Well, there isn't."

"What did Melvin the shaman tell you when you met him in Canada?" Seamus asked.

"He said you boys were fine, and everything was going fine, and there's nothing to worry about," Aaron

Finn said. "And he also said there was some kind of major calamity about to happen, the city of Los Angeles was in danger, and civilization as we know it might be coming to an end. Then he asked for an autographed picture of me. I gave him an eight-by-ten glossy."

"That's sort of a mixed message," Iggy said.

"We thought the same thing," Aaron Finn said. "But you know how these shamans are. They're cryptic."

My parents and my sister, Eloise, were sitting in a booth at the Brown Derby. Eloise was wearing sunglasses and had a scarf on her head. She held her hand out elegantly. "Mr. Finn, such a pleasure to see you again, and Billy, the specter—I hope you're both well. Hello, dear little brother, and your charming child friends."

"This place smells great," Billy said.

"I understand you have a part in a drama, Miss Eloise," Aaron Finn said.

"Oh, it's just a juvenile exercise," Eloise said. "A school play. But we actors must practice our art if we want to improve, as I am sure you agree."

"Oh, quite," Aaron Finn said. "I take a fencing lesson every day."

"Do you recommend that, Mr. Finn?" my sister asked. "I want to improve my craft."

"Oh, yes, I highly recommend fencing as exercise," Aaron Finn said. "And it's called for in roles surprisingly often."

"I will make a note of that," Eloise said. "And thank you for sharing such valuable information with a mere beginner."

It struck me as a little bit strange that Eloise was saying everything with an English accent—but then, many things she did were strange.

"Let's order," my father said. "And please notice, the waiter will come around with a pepper grinder the size of a baseball bat, and crank it right onto your salad."

My father ordered the Broiled Filet of Swordfish with Lemon Butter. My mother ordered the Scalloped Chicken Paprika with Noodles Polonaise. Eloise ordered Medallions of Lobster with Mushrooms, Queen of Sheba. Seamus, Iggy, Aaron Finn, and I ordered Spaghetti Derby, which is a specialty of the house—it turned out to be spaghetti in mushroom sauce, but it was pretty good. Billy sniffed everything.

"What's that horrible noise?" my mother asked.

We all heard it. It was a ghastly sucking, slurping, smacking kind of sound. Something about it made me cringe all up my spine. We looked around. At another table, a man was eating. He was pale and bald, and had a sort of egg-shaped head, gold-rimmed eyeglasses, and an expression that was between a crooked smile and a snarl. He had on an expensive-looking blue suit. There were three waiters hovering around his table as he hunched over a bowl of something, spooning it in and making those hideous noises.

"You know who that is?" Aaron Finn asked. I knew before he said it. "That gentleman is Sholmos Bunyip, head of International Mammon Studios, the most feared and hated man in Hollywood, and, I am sorry to say, my boss."

Sholmos Bunyip noticed Aaron Finn and sort of grunted in his direction. He wasn't looking directly at me, but I still felt a sick shiver.

Billy the Phantom Bellboy lifted his nose into the air and sniffed deeply. "You'll never guess what he's eating," Billy said.

I guessed. "Turtle soup?"

"You got it, Neddie," Billy said.

"He looks so . . . evil," my mother said.

"Could you introduce us?" Eloise said. "I'm sure it's not his fault that he looks like Satan, and maybe I could ask him to give me a job acting in a movie."

"It's not a good idea to approach him while he's eating," Aaron Finn said. "There's a story that he was on a hunting trip and shot one of his friends who came near him while he was having a sandwich."

Sholmos Bunyip had abandoned his spoon and was splashing the turtle soup into his mouth with his bare hands.

"Anyone for grapefruit cake?" Aaron Finn said. "It's a specialty of the house."

"Not for me," my father said.

"I think I need to get out in the air," my mother said.

"I may be sick," Iggy said.

"Of course," Aaron Finn said. "Excuse my insensitivity. It's a little shocking for regular people to see Mr. Bunyip. It doesn't bother actors, of course—we're used to frightening table manners."

CHAPTER 58

Night

When we got out of the Brown Derby, we were all sort of quiet. We were a little shaken. Seeing Sholmos Bunyip, in addition to being disgusting for the obvious reasons, had a bad effect on all of us. My Spaghetti Derby wasn't sitting well.

Seamus was going home with his father, so he wouldn't be staying on my bedporch. He went off in the Packard, and we Wentworthsteins, and Iggy, headed for the Hermione in the yellow Cadillac.

I had bad dreams. Sholmos Bunyip was in them. I woke up—it must have been around three in the morning. I wasn't scared the way you usually are when you wake up from a nightmare. In fact, I felt extremely calm. Then I did something I could never have explained.

I got out of bed. I moved through the dark apartment. In my pajamas, I went out into the corridor. I pressed the button for the elevator. I wasn't sure if I was really doing this or if it was another dream. I came out into the empty lobby, with half the lights turned off and the smell of freshly mopped floor. There was no one around.

I went out the side door, into the garden, and down along the side of the building. It was quiet outside in the dark. I made my way to the back of the building, past the incinerator and the garbage cans and into the thick weeds and scrub trees. It was as though I knew where I was going, but I didn't exactly.

There were the old abandoned tennis courts that nobody used anymore. And there was the old swimming pool. There were a few twigs and branches floating on top, and when I lowered myself in, I stood on a coating of soggy leaves. I swam out to the middle. The water was not too bad, fairly warm. It was a weird thing to do, getting into the old swimming pool in the middle of the night—but I somehow felt very satisfied, as if this was exactly where I belonged. I floated on my back and looked up at the stars. It was peaceful. It was more than peaceful. I was happy. I don't think I had ever been any happier.

Then I realized I wasn't alone. I wasn't the only

one swimming. It came up slowly, a dark shape in the darkness. Round. Huge. It rose up out of the water. I knew right away what it was.

I wasn't scared for a second. Just the opposite—I felt this tremendous . . . warmth. No, not warmth . . . joy. Oh, it was more than joy. It was . . . just the biggest kind of love. Love. This gigantic turtle, as big as a car, and so impossibly old, and I was brimming over with love for it.

And it loved me. I could see its old turtle head now, and its old turtle eye, could hear it breathing and feel it moving in the water right in front of me—and it was just radiating the purest kind of love. And it was wise. It knew everything, had seen everything— and it was telling me things—telling me things without words, things that couldn't be told in words. The best I can do—the best way I can translate what the great turtle told me—is to say that this is a beautiful world, and it wants to take care of us. I'm pretty sure I was crying.

We just floated there, the great turtle and me. It went on for a long time, maybe half an hour. Then the turtle sank down into the dark water. I climbed out of the pool, took off my pajamas and wrung them out, put them back on, and went back into the hotel.

CHAPTER 59

Rolling Doughnut

Iggy was sitting in the lobby when I came down.

"So, you ready to head for the Rolling Doughnut?" I asked her.

"That is no way to ask someone to go on a date," Iggy said.

"What date? It's Sunday morning. We always go to the Rolling Doughnut."

"Where is Seamus?" Iggy asked.

"He isn't here," I said.

"Right. So we are not going to the Rolling Doughnut as an acceptable group activity for young people. It's just you and me, so ask me properly."

This was not a problem for me, because I had read

that etiquette book in the Brown-Sparrow library. I bowed, and said, "Miss Yggdrasil, would you do me the honor of accompanying me to the Rolling Doughnut for an outdoor breakfast?"

"Yes, Mr. Neddie," Iggy said. "I would be pleased to be your guest at breakfast."

I offered Iggy my arm, and we went out the door.

"You understand, this means you pay," she said.

There were no customers when we arrived at the Rolling Doughnut. Instead of stepping up to the little window, Iggy went and sat at one of the picnic tables.

"Don't you want to order a doughnut and coffee?" I asked. She gave me a dirty look. "Oh. I get it. Miss Yggdrasil, may I offer you some refreshment?"

"Thank you, Mr. Neddie," Iggy said. "I will have a raspberry Bismarck and a medium coffee, black, please."

She's having a raspberry Bismarck? I thought to myself. When will this strange mood end? I got Iggy her Bismarck and coffee. For myself I chose the Hollywood health doughnut, whole-wheat with seeds, and a coffee with double cream and double sugar.

As we were eating our first doughnuts of the morning, I vaguely noticed two gray station wagons pulling up to the curb in the little side street beside the Rolling Doughnut. This was nothing especially interesting in itself. More interesting was that six fat men got out of each of the wagons.

All of them had suede shoes with thick crepe rubber soles, crewcuts, and plaid sport jackets. Also, they all wore horn-rimmed glasses, and had knitted neckties. I would say they all weighed about three hundred pounds and were of medium height. I couldn't say why, but I had the feeling that I had seen them somewhere before.

The twelve fat men all got two Bismarcks apiece, and cups of Postum, and carried them to the picnic tables. Two of them sat at the table to the right of ours, two of them sat at the table to the left, two at the table behind us, and two at the table in front. And four of them sat at our table, one on either side of Iggy, and one on either side of me!

"Do you mind if we sit here?" one of them asked, when they were already seated.

"Perfectly all right," I said.

"There's something funny about these guys," Iggy said.

"I know," I said. "They're cops of some sort." I didn't know why I said that, or how I knew it, but I did.

"Very astute, young man," one of the fat guys said.

"We are cops."

"Los Angeles cops?"

"No."

"State cops?"

"No."

"FBI?"

"Not that either."

"International Police?"

"You're getting warm."

"Wait! You don't mean to tell us that . . . "

The fat guy put his finger to his lips. "Let's just say that it took us quite a long time to get to this doughnut stand." He flipped open a wallet and showed me a badge made of some kind of green metal, and there was a card with his picture and writing in something that looked like Arabic or Hebrew, but it wasn't.

"We just want to ask a few questions. You're not in any trouble—with us," the fat policeman said.

CHAPTER 60

Just the Facts

"You're the kid with the turtle, right?" he asked me.

"Maybe I am," I said.

"Don't be cute with us, son," the fat cop from some other planet said. "Let's see the turtle."

"Better show him," Iggy said. "They weigh about two tons, collectively."

I dug out my turtle. The cop turned it over in his fingers. "What do you say, Frank? This the turtle?"

One of the other cops examined the turtle. "It's a clever copy, that's all," Frank said. "You can buy them like this for two space zlotys in that big drugstore on Spiegel 4."

"What about it, son?" the first cop asked me. "Is this the only turtle you've got?"

"Only one," I said.

"Where's the real one?"

"Not sure," I said.

"Think hard, punk," the fat cop said. "What's your best guess where it is?"

"We think a guy name of Sholmos Bunyip probably has it by now," I said.

"Lordbuckley! I hope he's wrong!" Frank said.

"Why? Would that be a bad thing?" I asked.

"This Bunyip is a fat cat and a bad hat," the cop said.

"If he has the turtle . . . well, your world might be more or less sort of doomed."

·· 239 ··

"I don't suppose you'd like to explain why," I said.

"I don't mind," the cop from space said. "You know—what is it—evolution?"

"Sure," I said.

"Well, we have reason to believe it might start going in the other direction, fast—and if it happens, it's going to start right here in L.A."

"I never heard of such a thing," I said.

"It's not all that common," the cop said. "But every so often, it tries to happen."

"Tries to?"

"Well, I'm no scientist," the cop said. "But there's

supposed to be someone equipped with that turtle we're talking about to keep things running in the usual direction, time-wise."

"That's what the turtle is for? How does it work?"

"As I said, I'm just a cop. We were led to believe you had the turtle and knew all about it."

"Are you going to take it away from Bunyip?" I asked. "He's supposed to be pretty evil."

"Oh, he's evil," the cop said. "But we can't take it away from him."

"Why not?"

"Well, we're cops. We can't go around taking people's property away. Did he steal the turtle?"

"No. I imagine he bought it," I said.

"Did the person he bought it from steal it?"

"No. I know he bought it," I said.

"Well, there you are. Anyway, it's not our jurisdiction. We're just here to get some facts. If there had been a problem, we would have told you to call the LAPD."

"So you're not going to do anything?"

"We are going to leave, is what we're going to do," the cop said. "Thanks for your cooperation, sir. Here is my card. Feel free to call me if you need anything, as soon as your planet gets interstellar phone service. And be on the lookout for glyptodons, saber-tooth cats, mammoths, and the like. If you see anything like that . . . well, good luck."

The cops bought four dozen Bismarcks, got into the two gray station wagons, and drove away.

Iggy and I looked at each other.

"You believe that?" I asked.

"I'm not sure," Iggy said. "You know, there are lots of weirdballs in Hollywood. And what was with the station wagons? Wouldn't you have expected space cops to turn up in a flying saucer or something? There was nothing about them that suggested any space man I ever heard of."

"They knew about the turtle," I said.

"Weren't you telling me that half the people you meet know about the turtle?" Iggy asked.

"This is true."

"I am withholding judgment until we get more information," Iggy said.

CHAPTER 61

More Information

"Look! Here comes the Leprechaun Man," Iggy said.

The Leprechaun Man was our name for one of the Hollywood weirdballs who came around the Rolling Doughnut fairly regularly. He always wore a blue blazer with brass buttons, and a ship captain's hat, and he talked to himself, mostly about the Little People.

"Aroo, arrah, it's the end of the world entirely," the Leprechaun Man said to no one in particular. "Whisht—it's bad cess to us all. We're banjaxed for a fact. There's to be lashings of giants, and ballyhooly, with the banshee screaming, bedad. And no one to help us but the Gentle People, macushla—or some similar crazy little eejits."

He got his doughnut and wandered off, mumbling and lilting.

"Proves nothing, one way or the other," I said. "He's always talking about disasters and giants and the Good Folk—besides, he's an utter loony."

"Sure and he is that," Iggy said.

CHAPTER 62

Who Else?

"I wonder who else will show up this morning," I said.

"My coffee got cold while those fat space cops were talking," Iggy said.

"I'll get you another one," I said.

Just then, Aaron Finn pulled up in his Packard convertible. Seamus and Billy the Phantom Bellboy were with him. "What ho, chaps?" Aaron Finn said.

"There were cops from space here," I said.

"Well, it was twelve fat guys who said they were space cops," Iggy put in.

"They said that Sholmos Bunyip was evil, and the world might be more or less sort of doomed."

"That could be serious," Aaron Finn said.

"They said it had to do with the turtle, in some

way that they didn't make clear," I said. "And it's a bad thing that Sholmos Bunyip has it. I feel sort of responsible."

"Oh, because you stashed the turtle at Stuffed Stuff 'n' Stuff?" Seamus said. "You shouldn't blame yourself, Neddie. It was a perfectly reasonable place to hide it."

"Is anybody getting doughnuts?" Billy the Phantom Bellboy asked. "I'm dying for a sniff."

"We should really have a talk with Sergeant Caleb, also known as Melvin the shaman," Aaron Finn said. "He's the one who gave you the turtle in the first place, and the only person I can think of who might know what it's all about."

"It's hard to get Melvin to give out information," Iggy said. "We tried one time, and it wasn't all that satisfactory. However, if you'd like to give it a shot, you may, because here he comes."

Sergeant Melvin was coming down the street. With him was Crazy Wig, wearing his horny hat.

"I thought you left town," I said to Crazy Wig.

"I got thrown off the bus for chanting and dancing," Crazy Wig said. "Do they have those twisted crullers here?"

"Allow me to shout for doughnuts for everybody," Aaron Finn said.

"Shout for?"

"It's Australian," Iggy said. "Means he's going to treat us. Make mine a double chocolate, please."

Aaron Finn made two trips with armloads of doughnuts and containers of coffee. "Now, Sergeant, what's the emmis?"

Melvin the sergeant took a sip of coffee. "You mean about the turtle?" he asked.

"Oooh! Oooh! I saw you in a vision," Crazy Wig said to Aaron Finn. "It was one of your past lives, without a doubt! It was sometime in the past, the Middle Ages, maybe. You had a sword, and you were fighting this guy with a big nose!"

"You're remembering a movie," I said. "He acts in movies."

"Oh," Crazy Wig said.

"Back to the turtle," Aaron Finn said. "Neddie tells us he talked to some policemen from another planet."

"Were they fat?" Melvin asked.

"Yes."

"I know those guys," Melvin the shaman said. "They have no jurisdiction in Los Angeles. They arrested my friend Crazy Wig here, and he just told them to take a walk."

"What did they arrest you for?" Seamus asked Crazy Wig.

"Predicting without a license," Crazy Wig said. "It was a bum rap. They didn't even know you don't need a license to make predictions on this planet. Some cops."

Aaron Finn was doing a good job of concealing the fact that he was getting frustrated. He was a good actor. "They told Neddie that the turtle, the original turtle you gave him, had something to do with a huge catastrophe that's supposed to happen."

"I don't see why that's any business of theirs," Melvin said. "They're not even from around here."

Seamus, Iggy, Billy the Phantom Bellboy, Crazy Wig, and I munched our doughnuts and enjoyed watching Aaron Finn try to interrogate Melvin the shaman.

"All right, let's take things one at a time," Aaron Finn said. "Is there going to be a catastrophe?"

"Well, sooner or later," Melvin said. "You wait around long enough, and everything will happen. Earthquakes, floods, forest fires, volcanic eruptions, plagues of giant animals—it's all part of life, you know. But you mustn't worry. Worrying never helps."

"We'll come back to the catastrophe," Aaron Finn said. "Let's talk about the turtle."

"What turtle?" Melvin asked.

"The one you gave Neddie."

"Oh yes, that turtle," Melvin said. "You know, he doesn't have it anymore."

"We know."

"To keep it safe, he switched it with another turtle at Stuffed Stuff 'n' Stuff, but unfortunately that man came in and bought it."

"That man? What man?"

"The one over there, ordering a doughnut."

Sandor Eucalyptus, also known as Nick Bluegum, was at the little window, buying two lemon-filled doughnuts and a grape soda.

"Seamus, go to the car and get my sword and my hat," Aaron Finn said. "Spread out, everyone. We're going to catch Mr. Eucalyptus."

Seamus hurried back with a sword, and a big hat with a feather. Aaron Finn put the hat on and took the sword in hand.

"Just like my vision!" Crazy Wig said.

CHAPTER 63

Neatly Done

It was neatly done. In a matter of seconds, Sandor Eucalyptus/Nick Bluegum was sitting spread eagle on one of the picnic benches, with his back against the table and each of his arms held by Melvin and Crazy Wig. Aaron Finn, in his big hat, had one foot on the bench and was bending with his face close to Bluegum's while tapping him on the shoulder with his sword.

"What is this? Unhand me!" Eucalyptus Bluegum said.

Aaron Finn laid the cool steel against Bluegum's cheek.

"We have you, my fine fellow," he said. "I'm sure you remember me from our airplane ride."

"Oh yes, my fellow tourist," Nick Bluegum said. "We had a nice time together, as I recall."

"Rat! You pulled a gun on me!" I said.

"But it wasn't a real gun," the sweating Eucalyptus said. "It only shoots little bits of potato. See for yourself—it's in my inside pocket."

Aaron Finn fished the gun out of Nick's pocket. "It's true. This is one of those potato guns," he said. "Just the same, you took this boy's turtle and jumped out of the airplane."

"I took a jellybean! Was that so wrong? Let me go!"

"What did you do with the turtle?" Aaron Finn asked, making his eyes narrow.

"It was a jellybean, I tell you. It took me a week to find my way out of the Grand Canyon, and it was the only thing I had to eat. Do you begrudge me a miserable jellybean?"

"This is getting us nowhere," Aaron Finn said. "Crazy Wig, commence the ceremonial torture."

"What? You're going to torture me at a doughnut stand in broad daylight?" Sandor Bluegum said.

"Are you sure?" Crazy Wig asked. "It's pretty disgusting to watch."

"Unless he talks," Aaron Finn said. "Do you have the angry scorpions and tinned anchovies?"

"I'll talk!" Nick Bluegum shouted.

"Fine," Aaron Finn said. "I suppose we can allow our guest to be comfortable—let go his arms, fellows. But remember, Bluegum, I can run you through in a second."

"I know," Nick Bluegum said. "I've seen you kill Basil Rathbone in lots of movies."

Melvin and Crazy Wig released Bluegum's arms and handed him his grape soda.

"Ask him why he tried to hold me up in the airplane," I said.

"Someone took a bite out of my lemon-filled doughnut," Bluegum said.

"Talk," Aaron Finn said.

"I had no choice," Bluegum said. "He told me to get the turtle."

"He?"

"He."

"Are you referring to Sholmos Bunyip?"

"Shhh!" Bluegum shuddered. "Don't say his name."

"How did you know I had it?"

"That man told me."

"Melvin?"

"Yes. I ran into him in a lunchwagon in Winslow, Arizona."

"Melvin, you told him?"

"Well, I might have mentioned it," Melvin the shaman said.

"Why would you do a thing like that?"

"I don't know—can't keep a secret, I guess. It's a big fault, especially if you're a shaman."

"So I decided I would steal it," Sandor Eucalyptus said. "And please my master."

"Sholmos."

"Shhh!"

"And then you bought the turtle from Steve Kraft at Stuffed Stuff 'n' Stuff."

"Yes, but that's a fake one. He made it himself. I was so afraid of you-know-who . . . I hoped it would fool him."

"And did it?"

"It did at first. But he's clever—he checks up on me. He found out where I got it, knows I handed him a fake. Now I'm sure he's after me. If he was to catch up with me, you could do me a favor and stick that sword right through me."

"Why did Sholmos Bunyip—?" Aaron Finn began.

"Shhh!"

"Why did you-know-who want the turtle to begin with?"

"He didn't want it for himself. He was getting it for his master."

"His master?"

"Yes. You-know-who is my master, and bosses me around and frightens me—and in turn there is someone who bosses and frightens him."

"That must be a pretty bad someone," Aaron Finn said.

CHAPTER 64

Good Old Packard

"So Bluegum and Bunyip don't know they got the authentic turtle," Seamus whispered to me.

"Not yet," I whispered back.

Nick Bluegum was saying, "Bring on the scorpions and anchovies. I am not saying another word."

"He's too scared to mention who it is that Sholmos Bunyip is scared of," Iggy said.

"Ah, there you are!" a voice said. "I was hoping I'd find you." It was Al Crane.

"Hello, Al," Seamus said. "See that guy? He's the one who tried to hold up Neddie for the turtle, and later bought it from Steve Kraft, but he doesn't know it's the real one. We've been trying to get him to talk.

He told us some stuff, but now he's clammed up. I don't think wild elephants could get another word out of him."

"Funny you should mention that," Al said. "Could I interest everybody in coming out to the farm? Something pretty interesting has come up."

"I'll ask my father," Seamus said. "Father, Al here wants us to come out to the San Fernando Valley to see something pretty interesting." Then he added in a whisper, "They have lions out there. Maybe we can threaten Bluegum with them."

"There's only so far we can go with this sort of thing," Aaron Finn whispered. "I think it may be against the law to torture people, even if you're a movie star and a Republican. But . . . let's go anyway. A drive in the country will be nice. Let's go, everybody. Plenty of room in the car!"

Good old Packard! We all fit. Melvin and Crazy Wig sat on either side of Nick Bluegum. Crazy Wig had the potato gun pointed at him. On the way, Iggy, Seamus, and I filled Al in on what had been happening. Al, for his part, refused to tell us what interesting thing had come up out at the circus winter quarters.

"This is kidnapping, you know," Nick Bluegum said.

"I believe the police at the Grand Canyon are looking for you," Aaron Finn said. "So this is a citizen's arrest. You did commit armed robbery, after all."

"It was a potato gun, and I took a jellybean!" Nick Bluegum said.

"Don't forget, you also stole a valuable parachute," I said.

"Wait a minute! Where's Billy?" Iggy said. We looked around. Sometimes Billy is hard to see.

"I don't think he's with us," Seamus said.

"Could we have left him behind at the Rolling Doughnut?" I asked.

"If you mean that semitransparent chap, I saw him leave while you were intimidating me," Nick Bluegum said.

"Odd. Where can he have gone?" Aaron Finn said. "Well, he's a grown ghost and knows what he's doing. No doubt he'll turn up."

CHAPTER 65

Something Fairly Interesting

There was no trouble guessing what Al Crane wanted to show us when we got to the farm. We could see it towering over everything else as soon as we drove through the gate.

"What is that!?!" we all asked, although it was perfectly obvious what it was—obvious, but unbelievable.

"This," Al said, "is a mammoth." He was smiling and beaming.

"It is! It actually is!" we all said.

"It's an imperial mammoth, and he's ours—that is, he belongs to this circus. Nobody else has got one."

Bobby, the elephant trainer, was in the enclosure with the imperial mammoth, petting him and looking at him with eyes brimming with happiness. "He's a good boy," Bobby was saying over and over.

"But these are extinct," Iggy said.

"So it was generally believed," Al said. "But here he is. His name is Don. That's short for Archidiskodon, his scientific handle—*Archidiskodon imperator*. He's a beauty, is he not?"

"I mean . . . how? Why? Where did you get him?"

"We found him," Bobby said. "Just found him wandering in the fields. Finders keepers, of course. He's a circus mammoth now, aren't you, Donny boy?"

The mammoth was quite a bit taller than the tallest elephant, and had a set of tusks that went on and on. The regular elephants were huddled together in another corral, looking at Don with unbelieving expressions.

"You found a mammoth, an animal supposed to be extinct for the last ten thousand years, just wandering around?" I asked.

"He was eating grass," Bobby said. "He's a nice mammoth." Bobby kissed the mammoth on the knee.

"Piece of luck, huh?" Al said.

"Don't you find this a bit strange?" Seamus asked.

"Strange? It's flipping incredible!" Al said. "Imagine how he's going to look leading the circus parade. My father and Clive Montague are on the phone with the lady who makes the elephant costumes for us right now."

Melvin the shaman and Crazy Wig had sat down on the ground and were rocking back and forth, eyes closed, chanting in some language I'd never heard before. The rest of us were milling around in front of the enclosure, looking at Don the mammoth and trying to get our brains to believe what our eyes were telling them.

Except for Sandor Eucalyptus, a.k.a. Nick Bluegum. He was standing stock-still, white as a sheet, eyes wide and mouth hanging open. "It has begun," he said.

"I beg your pardon?" Aaron Finn asked. "What has begun?"

Sandor Bluegum clutched the sleeve of Aaron Finn's expensive movie star jacket. "I'll tell you what has begun. I want to tell you everything."

"Now you're showing good sense," Aaron Finn said. "Come, sit on this bench, under this tree. Everybody! Gather round. Mr. Bluegum is going to tell us everything."

"We have to finish our death chant," Melvin said. "We'll join you in a few minutes."

"I wonder if I might have a cold drink," Nick Bluegum said. "A grape soda, if possible."

"There's a cooler outside the bunkhouse," Al said. "I'll see what we have. Anybody else want something? Don't start until I get back."

"Do I need to listen to this?" Bobby the elephant trainer asked. "I'd prefer to stay with Don."

Al arrived with an armload of bottles of soda, cold and dripping from the cooler, and Aaron Finn opened them with his gold-plated Boy Scout knife. Melvin and Crazy Wig had finished singing the death chant and walked over, dusting off their clothes. We all settled down, some sitting on the ground, around the bench under the tree and listened to Nick Bluegum.

CHAPTER 66

A Terrifying Story

"I have a terrifying story to tell," Nick Bluegum began. We sipped our cold sodas and listened.

"First, I must tell you that Sholmos Bunyip is a being of pure evil, a monster."

"Well, come to it, all the studio heads are like that," Aaron Finn said. "Cecil B. De Mille, Louis B. Mayer, Walt B. Disney—monsters one and all."

"Bunyip is worse," Nick Bluegum said.

"Worse than Walt Disney?" Aaron Finn asked.

"I tell you, he is evil beyond your wildest imaginings," Nick Bluegum said.

"We know his son," Seamus Finn whispered to his father. "He's extremely evil, considering he's no older than I am."

"I was not always bad," Nick Bluegum said. "I was a lovely, sensitive boy. I loved nature. I spent many happy hours yodeling and picking wildflowers in my native country, the Duchy of Botstein. My people were humble craftsmen who wove shoelaces by hand for the simple people of our village."

"That's a coincidence," I said. "My father makes shoelaces."

"Who does not know of Roger Wentworthstein, the shoelace king?" Nick Bluegum said. "It pained me all the more to have to pull a potato gun on the son of such a great man. But, you see, I had no choice. I had become a veritable slave to the evil Bunyip. At first I was happy. It was my job to clean and polish the many light bulbs used in the production of motion pictures. I was good at my work, and wanted no more.

"Then Bunyip drew me to him. At first, he was nice to me. He bought me liverwurst sandwiches in the studio cafeteria. Naturally, when he asked me to run little errands for him, I was happy to oblige. He always gave me a dime when I went to the drugstore for him, brought him mints—then he would give me a quarter. And soon, he owned my soul. Soon, hungry for tips, and then afraid of his anger, I would do his evil bidding in anything."

"This is boring," Iggy said. "Get to the point."

"This is the point—have you ever wondered how Sholmos Bunyip rose to such wealth and power?"

"Cheating, stealing, and yelling at people?" Aaron Finn suggested.

"No! He has a powerful confederate," Nick Bluegum said. "Bunyip is the servant of an ancient prehistoric earth spirit whose name I shudder to pronounce."

"Can you spell it?" Aaron Finn asked.

"No. It is Kkhkktonos," Nick Bluegum said, making a noise like preparing to spit. "There is a little turtle pond behind Sholmos Bunyip's office, and it is there, at night, that Kkhkktonos appears to him. Kkhkktonos is an earth-god, from a time before humans. He had great power, but he lost most of it when the last ice age ended. But he was still able to do little favors for Bunyip—in much the way Bunyip did little favors for me. Thus was Bunyip able to become great, and run a movie studio, and push people around, and have three swimming pools."

"But Kkhkktonos wanted something in return!" Iggy said.

"But Kkhkktonos wanted something in return," Nick Bluegum said.

"I know! I know! Kkhkktonos wants to bring back the ice age!" Iggy said, excited.

"Who's telling this, you or me?" Nick Bluegum

said. "Yes. Kkhkktonos wanted to bring back his days of greatness, and power—but first someone, Bunyip, had to get the sacred turtle for him."

"Now that's the part we're all interested in," Aaron Finn said. "What does the turtle have to do with all this?"

"It is foretold that the one in possession of the sacred turtle can defeat the earth-gods and prevent the resurgence of the days of Kkhkktonos's power," Nick Bluegum said. "Apparently, through the millennia, every few hundred years, the old powers try to come back, and always there is some hero, always with that little turtle, who stops it from happening."

"And if Sholmos Bunyip had the turtle, there would be no one to stop it this time," I said.

"Exactly."

"Melvin, did you know about all this when you gave me the turtle?" I asked Melvin.

"I think I knew about it at one time, and then forgot," Melvin said. "It all sounds very familiar."

"And, of course, the presence of that imperial mammoth over there . . . " Seamus said.

"Means it has started already," Nick Bluegum said. "Young Neddie Wentworthstein, do you have the turtle?"

"Actually, no," I said.

"Then we are all doomed."

"Yep, that's how it looks to me too," Melvin said. "I'm sorry to have to break this up, but it's time I went on duty at the school. Mr. Finn, could I trouble you for a ride back to town?"

CHAPTER 67

Gave It Away

Al stayed behind at the circus farm. The last thing he said was "So, if I understand this correctly, there may soon be more ice age animals for us to catch? Neat!"

In the car I asked, "What can we do about this?"

"Oh, I wouldn't plan to do anything, Neddie," Melvin said.

"You wouldn't?" Iggy asked him.

"Oh, no. And I wouldn't worry either. It never helps to worry."

When we got back to the Hermione, after dropping Melvin the shaman off at Brown-Sparrow, Billy the Phantom Bellboy was haunting the lobby.

"Guess where I've been," he said.

"We saw a mammoth," I said. "And we found out that evolution might start running backwards, and we'll be living in the ice age, and Sholmos Bunyip works for a prehistoric earth-god named Kkhkktonos, and the world as we know it might sort of be ending."

"I've been visiting Sholmos Bunyip," Billy said.

"You've been what?"

"I went over and observed him. Just walked right in, invisible. I know what's going on—the whole megillah—and I can tell you, I was never happier to be dead."

"It's bad?"

·· 267 ··

"Depends how you look at it. Bad for you life-os, certainly. But only temporarily."

"How so?"

"Well, you'll be like me pretty soon, I expect. It's not so bad, really—of course, you'll miss having solid bodies, and food, and sleep, and since everybody else will be ghosts too, there will be no one to haunt. I guess we'll have to haunt each other."

"You want to get specific?"

"Well, in a nutshell, Sholmos Bunyip is not only bad, but also crazy and stupid—put this together with always having his own way, and you have a recipe for disaster. He has somehow hooked up with this . . . thing. I don't know how to describe it—it's like the devil, only I always pictured the devil as nicer."

"This is Kkhkktonos you're talking about?"

"That's the one! He . . . it . . . whatever, was the head spirit for thousands and thousands of years. Sort of sank out of sight as the last ice age ended. During the period when he was in charge, it was all things eating things, and blood and violence, and sharp claws and crunching teeth. Personally, I don't see the appeal, but Kkhkktonos wants to bring it all back, and the idiot Bunyip, who is only going to get eaten himself, is helping him do it.

"Here's how it works—Kkhkktonos is underground, literally. He lurks around deep in the earth. There are a couple of places where he comes to the surface. One is the La Brea Tar Pits. Did you know that 'La Brea' means 'the tar' in Spanish, so when you say 'the La Brea Tar Pits' you're actually saying 'the the tar tar pits'? Anyway, he can make his way to the surface there, and also through a small turtle pond outside Sholmos Bunyip's office at the studio. Bunyip goes down there and makes kissy-kissy noises, and Kkhkktonos rants and raves, and promises Bunyip he will rule as a king, and tells him what to do.

"By the way, Bunyip's collection of turtle art, and

his turtle shrine and turtle zoo, are pretty impressive. He'd have been after that turtle of yours, Neddie, even if he wasn't hooked up with the old earth-demon.

"Kkhkktonos can't do much for himself. His powers have diminished, I guess because he was left behind by evolution, but he's still able to dominate the weak-minded studio chief Bunyip.

"Now, it turns out there is a periodic natural event—think of it as a volcanic eruption—when a sort of pressure builds up, and Kkhkktonos, and I suppose there are other prehistoric earth-gods or powers, sort of try to bust out, and with them come glaciers, and actual volcanos, and your saber-tooth cats and giant sloths, and so on."

"And one of those events is fixing to happen," I said.

"More than fixing to, I think," Billy said. "It may be by way of happening, or starting to happen, already. Hence that mammoth you were talking about."

"And is there anything to stop this?" I asked.

"I was coming to that. It's all up to some designated hero—there's always a designated hero—and you can tell who he is because he has a certain sacred turtle."

"I guess that was supposed to be me, only now I have no idea what to do."

"Plus, you don't have the turtle," Billy said.

"Bunyip has it," I said.

"Bunyip had it," Billy said. "You know, he was sure Nick Bluegum had fobbed off a fake on him, when it was the real turtle all along."

"He still doesn't know he has the real one?"

"He doesn't even have it. As far as I could tell, he gave it to some kid. But Bunyip and Kkhkktonos think you don't have it either, plus, as you pointed out, you have no idea what you're supposed to do, and they know this."

"So they're going ahead with the de-evolution thing?"

"It's going to happen no matter what they do. Bunyip is just going to help Kkhkktonos so he can be the head devil when it is all done happening."

"Oh, woe is us," Crazy Wig said.

"You can say that again, brother," Billy said.

"Oh, woe is us."

CHAPTER 68

Shoe-la Hoop

My father came out of the elevator. "Oh, Neddie! There you are! And all your friends. I was hoping to meet you. I want you to look at this." He had a cardboard carton with him. Out of it he pulled a multicolored tangled thing. "I just invented this. It's a new kind of toy. It's going to be a fantastic sensation, the next yo-yo."

"It looks like some kind of lasso," Iggy said.

"It has things in common with the lasso, or lariat, or throwing rope," my father said. "You've all seen cowboys in movies doing fancy rope tricks."

"I can do a few myself," Iggy said.

"Then you know they're very hard to learn," my father said. "With my invention, which I call the Shoe-la Hoop—it's made of shoelaces—anyone can do rope tricks, just like the cowboys. Here, little Yggdrasil, and Neddie, and Seamus, here are Shoe-la Hoops. Try them out. You see, the woven shoelaces keep the hoop in shape, and you can swing it around your shoulders, your waist, your hips, your wrists or ankles."

For a moment, I considered telling my father about the ice age coming back, and the world being dominated by the unspeakably evil Kkhkktonos, and saber-tooth cats eating people alive on Hollywood Boulevard—but what good would it have done? Besides, those things seemed sort of unreal, remote and far away . . . and also, for some reason, I wasn't all that worried. Melvin had said not to worry. He said worrying never helped. And the truth was, ever since I had met the great turtle in the deserted swimming pool, I'd had this calm, happy feeling that nothing could shake. The other kids, and Aaron Finn, and Billy, and Crazy Wig, all seemed to be in a similar mood somehow. Even Nick Bluegum, formerly the stooge of the evil Bunyip, was interested in the Shoe-la Hoop, and didn't seem to be thinking about all the horrible catastrophe stuff that was supposed to happen.

So, we all took turns learning to work the Shoe-la Hoops, there in the lobby of the Hermione Hotel, on the eve of total destruction.

CHAPTER 69

Nothing

Nothing happened over the next few days. That is, nothing abnormal or unnatural. I went to school—the usual kids were there. I hung around with my friends after school. My family carried on with life as usual. Except for Don the mammoth, I knew of no other Pleistocene animals turning up.

More days passed. We went out to the circus farm a couple of times and watched them training Don, there was a swim meet against Black-Foxe, the other military school in town, we studied ancient Rome in Miss Magistra's class, we ate doughnuts. Sergeant Melvin was at his post, hollering at us to button our buttons and walk in a military manner, and suggesting jazz musicians to listen to in the booths at the music store.

The whole idea of there being some kind of pre-historic devil trying to make a comeback, and de-evolution to the ice age, started to blend with things like the Japanese ghosts nobody ever saw in the pagoda at school, or the plots of serials we saw at the Hitching Post theater. Al had never acted as though he thought it was anything else—just a good imaginary game he was going along with.

I even thought that perhaps Don the mammoth was just the last of his kind, wandering around the San Fernando Valley without anyone ever noticing him, until the circus people found him. Such things happen. There are holdovers and throwbacks. Cadet Bruce Bunyip, for example, was a whole lot like a Neanderthal, if you went by the pictures in the Natural Sciences textbook.

"Hello, fellows," Bunyip said to Seamus, Al, and me. He was chewing some tar he had pulled up from the road.

"Go away, Bunyip," we said. "We just had lunch, and you might make us lose our Spam."

"You guys are not afraid of me. I like that," Bunyip said. "And sometimes you are nice to me."

"Are you referring to the time I threw a tennis ball and let you fetch it?" Al asked.

"Look what I have," Bunyip said. He was tossing

a small object in his palm. It was the turtle! The original sacred turtle!

"Where did you get that?" Seamus asked.

"Father gave it to me. It's real old. I'm going to drill a hole in it and keep it on my key chain."

"Say, may I see it?" I asked.

Bunyip hesitated.

"Show your turtle to Cadet Wentworthstein," Seamus said. "He will give it right back."

"Promise?" Bunyip asked.

"I'll just look at it and plunk it right back into your paw," I said.

Bunyip handed me the turtle.

"Look! Is that an eagle?" Seamus shouted, pointing into the sky.

Bunyip looked up while I made the switch, but it wasn't necessary—I did the French substitution so smoothly, even Seamus wouldn't have spotted it.

"No, I was mistaken. Not an eagle," Seamus said.

"Aww, too bad. I wanted to see an eagle," Bunyip said.

Sometimes I felt sorry for Bunyip. Then he would bash someone in the nose, or bite someone, and I would get over it. I plunked the fake turtle into his sweaty palm. The real one was in my pocket! I had it back!

"My father is going to do something nice for the whole school," Bunyip said.

"What is that, transfer you someplace else?"

"He is going to invite the whole school to see a circus," Bunyip said.

"It's true," Al said. "Sholmos Bunyip is hiring the Gibbs Brothers Circus for a special performance. I heard my father telling my mother."

"I have to go threaten some third-graders," Bunyip said. "You want to come and watch?"

"No, you go ahead and have fun," we said. Bunyip loped off evilly.

"There goes a slow-witted bully we can be proud of," Seamus said.

"Yes, he's a fine boy in his very special way," I said.

"It wouldn't be the same without him," Al said.

CHAPTER 70

Turtle, Turtle, Who's Got the Turtle?

"I have the turtle back," I told Sergeant Melvin.

"See? I told you not to worry," Melvin said.

"Seamus Finn knows I have it. I'm not telling anyone else, except you."

"That's probably a good idea," Melvin the shaman said. "I will make a point of trying to remember not to tell anyone you have it."

"Oh! I forgot," I said. "You can't keep a secret, can you?"

"No. I'm just a blabbermouth," Melvin said. "But I'll make a special effort if you don't want me to tell."

"The reason I mention it at all," I said, "is that I still don't know what I'm supposed to do with it."

"Do with it?"

"In the event . . . if things should happen . . . if that stuff we were talking about, the ice age coming back, and that old-time earth-god . . . what I'm supposed to do then."

"Have you seen any signs of things like that starting to happen?"

"Well, except for Don the mammoth turning up, not really."

"So, why worry about it?" Melvin asked. "It may never happen."

"You don't know what I'm supposed to do—with the turtle, I mean—do you?"

"It's perfectly simple. If that thing you were talking about—where the old powers try to come back, and the planet is plunged into chaos, and civilization is destroyed, and it gets all violent and evil—if that was to start happening, the old legends tell that a hero, identified by his connection with the sacred turtle, always stops it, so the normal order of things can continue."

"Yes, I get that. But how? How does he do it? And am I that guy?"

"Well, you have the turtle. I guess if it happens while you have it—happens on your watch—then you are the guy."

"When you had the turtle, before you gave it to me, were you the guy?"

"Interesting question. No, I don't think I was. I think I had the turtle so I could give it to you."

"Can I give the turtle to someone else? Can I give it to someone more heroic, like Clive Montague? Can I give it to you?"

"No. You have to keep it. You can pass it on to another only when the turtle itself tells you to do that."

"Did the turtle itself tell you to give it to me?"

"Must have. I gave it to you, didn't I?"

"And you're sure you gave it to the right person."

"I'm a qualified shaman. I wouldn't make a mistake about a thing like that."

"Okay, okay, now listen carefully. What exactly would I be supposed to do, assuming I am the guy who is supposed to have the turtle? What would I be supposed to do if the deal where evolution goes backwards and all that happens? That is what I am asking you."

"Don't worry, Neddie. You always worry. A hero knows. He knows what to do. That's why he's a hero."

"So I'm a hero?"

"You will be if you save civilization."

Then Sergeant Caleb told me to put my hat on straight, and hurry to my next class.

CHAPTER 71

I Have the Turtle

That night I went down to the deserted swimming pool behind the hotel. This time I was not in my pajamas, and I didn't actually get into the water. I sat cross-legged by the side of the pool, and waited. I didn't have to wait long. The black dome of his shell rose above the surface, and I felt joy rise in my heart.

He was bigger than he had seemed the first time I saw him. It was no trouble for him to step onto the poolside tiles and haul himself out of the water. The great turtle towered over me. Then he settled down beside me, his great feet tucked under him, and I caught the glint of his wise eyes in the light of a street lamp that shone through the trees.

It was beautiful listening to him breathe. I

breathed too, and I knew he was listening to me. After a while, we began to breathe a song. Old song. Oldest song ever. It went on for a long time. The song was showing me things, teaching me things. I became aware that I knew things I had always known, and things I had never known before. I saw back in time, saw the whole life of the turtle, and all turtles. I saw a world that no longer existed, under a sun that had not shone for thousands of years.

There were things about me too. I had done this before. The turtle had always been my friend. In some strange way, I was as old as the turtle, and he was as old as creation. We sang. We breathed. Our breaths and our song were part of a bigger song that everything in the world was singing, was always singing, had always sung.

At one point, the great turtle rested his huge old head on my knee. I put my hand on his head, and my eyes filled with tears.

"Thank you, turtle," I whispered. "Thank you, Grandfather."

He slid into the water and sank out of sight.

CHAPTER 72

The School Outing

"Put on your Windbreakers," Miss Magistra said first thing in the morning when we came to class. "Go directly to the parade ground, and form ranks. There is a surprise for you today." Bunyip and Al Crane were not in class. I thought I knew where they were, and I was pretty sure I knew what the surprise was.

There were buses on the parade ground, and Colonel Groscase, wearing his beautiful camelhair colonel coat. "Cadets, you get a treat today," Colonel Groscase bellowed. "The great studio executive Sholmos Bunyip, father of our own popular Cadet Bunyip, has invited the entire school to a circus! You will board the buses by platoons, in an orderly fashion. There will be no singing, shouting, or exposing of backsides out the bus windows. Upon arrival at the studio, you will disembark the buses. Studio employees will give you special garments, which you will put on over your uniforms. You will then be directed to your seats, where you will enjoy the circus, applaud, cheer, and wave your arms. Company commanders, direct the cadets to board the buses!"

"Special garments? What's that about?" I asked Seamus Finn.

"No idea, old pal," Seamus Finn said.

When we got to International Mammon Studios, the buses pulled up outside the life-size Roman Coliseum, which I had watched being built a long way off from my window.

We knew all about the Coliseum because we had studied ancient Rome in Miss Magistra's class. For example, I knew that the Romans didn't call it the Coliseum—its name was the Flavian Amphitheatre, and it was built between A.D. 70 and A.D. 80. It could seat at least forty-five thousand people, and it had a movable roof, called the velarium, which was rigged like sails, and raised and lowered by sailors. Also, they could flood the arena, and it was big enough to stage naval battles. The reason the Coliseum is not one of the

Wonders of the Ancient World is that the list was composed in the third century B.C., more than two hundred years before it was built. Otherwise, it would have been number eight for sure.

They had chariot races, and gladiators fighting— which was sort of sick because they had real swords and spears—and sicker yet was turning wild animals, like lions and tigers, loose on people. However, it was a lot of fun to read about.

As we got off the bus, studio employees handed us togas and told us to put them on. Togas? We pulled them on over our uniforms. It was sort of neat, to be going into the fake Coliseum dressed up as fake Romans.

"I am Julius Greaser," Cadet Merriwell said.

"Friends, Romans, countrymen, lend me a dollar until Thursday," Cadet Burns said.

"*Veni, vidi, vici*—I have to go weewee," Cadet Terwilliger said.

"*Omnia Gallia in tres partes divisa est,*" Cadet Stover said, which was only slightly less funny than what the other kids said, and showed off that he could actually say a sentence in Latin.

"Overstay isay ayay oopyheadpay," Cadet McCoy said.

"I bet anything there will be cameras facing the audience," Seamus Finn said.

"This thing is life-size," I said. "You think they invited forty-five thousand people to see the circus?"

By this time we were being herded up the ramps and through the corridors, then through tunnels that led into the amphitheater. When we came out into the stands, we all said the same thing. "Wow!" is what we said.

CHAPTER 73

Wow!

The stands were almost full. It was a sea of people in togas. And, just as Seamus had predicted, there were cameras on cranes, lenses aimed at the audience. The studio employees directed us to a section with the words "Brown-Sparrow" taped to the seatbacks. They were good seats, right down in front. We'd get a good view of everything.

It looked as though everyone in Los Angeles were there. We could see where the kids from the Harmonious Reality School, Iggy's school, were sitting. They had drawn flowers on their togas with crayons and poster paint, and were holding up a banner that said NOSCE TE IPSUM. Crazy Wig was in the crowd, wearing his toga, and also his fur hat with the buffalo horns.

High up in the stands, I saw a bunch of fat guys— their horn-rimmed glasses reflecting the sun—it had to be those cops from outer space.

There were vendors moving through the crowd selling sausages. The pretty actress whose life had been ruined by Sholmos Bunyip was selling Roman doughnuts. And I heard my father's voice shouting, "*Ligula, ligula, ligula!* Get your Imperial Shoe-la Hoops! *Ludere, ludere, ludere!*" My mother was selling them too. There were balloon vendors, and guys selling cups of orange juice. The Leprechaun Man was wandering up and down the stadium steps, talking to himself about the Little People.

Everybody was cheering and hollering. The Brown-Sparrow band, wearing togas and shiny gold helmets, was on the field, marching and playing.

On the special platform called the *suggestum,* where the emperor sat, was Sholmos Bunyip, with the odious Bruce beside him, the two of them surrounded by movie stars. He waved his hand, the Brown-Sparrow band marched off the field, and a bunch of guys with tremendous trumpets came out and blew a fanfare. Then Sholmos Bunyip stood up, and spoke into an ancient Roman microphone. We heard his voice over loudspeakers. "Let the games begin!" he said.

CHAPTER 74

The Games Begin

First came the circus parade. Clowns first, lots of them, slapping their big shoes on the sand, pushing baby carriages with little clowns in them, slapping each other with slapsticks, stumbling and bumping into one another, doing somersaults and cartwheels. Great clowns! Then there were horses, beautiful circus horses, with bareback-riding ladies in sequined tights. Camels came out, with bright red cloths trimmed with jingle bells over their humps. Then acrobats, tumbling and jumping.

The arena was filling with people in sparkling costumes, animals—and then the elephant parade! Sixteen elephants, each holding the tail of the elephant before it in its trunk—the biggest elephant first, and at the end a baby elephant—lumbered around the arena. And there was a calliope playing! A steam calliope! This is the most amazing, most unexpected musical instrument ever. It's like an organ, and at the same time it's like huge whistles, and it's played with a keyboard like a piano, and it's run by steam pressure, and it's loud, and it has a beautiful hollow hooting-whistling sound that's not like anything else in the world.

"This is good," I said to Seamus Finn. "You know, Sholmos Bunyip is obviously evil and everything, but it's pretty nice of him to throw this free circus for everybody."

"It's also a lot cheaper to hire the circus for a day than pay forty-five thousand extras," Seamus said. "That's what the cameras are for."

"Oh," I said.

"Obviously they're making a movie set in ancient Rome, and they need shots of the audience for some scene set in the Coliseum. Pretty clever trick, huh?"

Just then, through the doors at one end of the arena, came Don the mammoth, all by himself. And riding on his head was our boy Al! The crowd gasped when they saw Don, saw how inconceivably big he was—there was complete silence as he walked out into the middle of the ring. And then everybody went wild.

The Brown-Sparrow cadets went even wilder. I am sure not one kid, except for Seamus and me, knew that Al Crane, the quiet little guy that nobody paid attention to, was with the circus. He had on a great costume, with a gold turban, and when he made Don the mammoth do a walk around the whole arena, he stood up on the huge head and bowed as he passed our part of the stands. Kids were yelling and yelling his name, and throwing their hats in the air. Al was smiling a big smile.

It was hard to believe that the actual show would be better than the parade—but it was. Great tall poles, steadied by guy wires, had been set up to support the trapezes and the high wire. The aerialists climbed and climbed up long ladders, and we held our breath, and they swung and flew without a net. The wirewalkers were balancing so far up, we had to bend our necks all the way back to watch them. The trapeze artists were swinging and catching each other. The calliope was playing.

And then lions appeared out of trapdoors in the floor. This was a special feature of the Coliseum. They used to have lions and other wild animals pop out of trapdoors for the purpose of fighting with gladiators and eating unfortunates who had been captured in wars, or were disliked by the emperor.

But these lions were not going to eat anyone—we hoped. They were not inside a cage, though, as they would have been in a regular circus. The parapet around the arena was built to the same height as the original Roman one, and that had been scientifically designed to be just barely too high for the average lion to jump up into the seats and eat people. So Clive Montague was able to do his act with the lions running loose all around the arena, which they seemed to be enjoying. It was really impressive, because the lions could get away from him if they wanted to. Also, he did not have the option of running outside the cage if they got feisty.

And, sure enough, some of the lions tried to jump up the wall and join the audience—and it looked like they could almost make it. All this was going on while the aerial acrobats were up there doing their stuff, and Clive was the only human on the floor of the arena. It was exciting and scary, and pretty incredible that he was able to get all the big cats to perch on their stands, jump through hoops, come to him when called, and allow him to play with them and put his hands in their mouths. He didn't put his head in a lion's mouth, but that was a tiny defect in an otherwise highly satisfactory performance.

Pretty Good Show

This had to be better than the Roman circus, and we didn't have to watch anybody get eaten, which I considered a plus, though some cadets expressed an opposite opinion.

"Pretty good show." A voice in my ear. It was Billy the Phantom Bellboy, sitting next to me, completely invisible.

Clive Montague had chased the lions into their chute, the acrobats were climbing down the ladders, and they were getting ready for the chariot race.

"Did you know that in Roman times, they could flood the arena floor?" Billy asked me.

I knew that.

"Did you know this one is built just the same?"

"Been doing more snooping?" I asked Billy.

"I have," Billy said. "And did you know that Sholmos Bunyip has had a tunnel built that connects the arena to the turtle pond behind his office?"

"Why would he do that? Wait! The turtle pond where he communicates with Kkhkktonos?"

"Yep," Billy said. "The only two places where the nasty old earth-god seems able to emerge from underground are that pond and the La Brea Tar Pits."

"And now he will be able to emerge here," I said.

"And did you know that there's a full moon tonight?" I knew that.

"But did you know that this will be the twelve thousandth full moon since the last time it happened?"

"It? Happened?"

"It."

"Happened?"

"Well, tried to happen. The resurgence of the old nonorder," Billy said. "You know, the thing Kkhkktonos wants to happen, where civilization is gone in a flash and life is all about mean big animals crunching little weaker animals in their jaws, and Kkhkktonos reigns supreme. Bunyip thinks Kkhkktonos is going to make him king of all creation, but I bet he gets eaten in the first fifteen minutes."

"Wait, and you're saying that the twelve thou-sandth full moon since the last time . . . "

"Means you're on, Neddie. Tonight, you get to do your stuff."

"You sure about this?" I asked Billy.

"Fairly sure."

"How come Melvin didn't tell me about this?" I asked.

"I dunno. Maybe he forgot," Billy said.

CHAPTER 76

He Forgot?

The chariot race was exciting, but I was distracted and couldn't fully enjoy it. When it was over, Sholmos Bunyip spoke into the ancient Roman microphone again. "This concludes the circus. International Mammon Studios thanks you for your attendance. The next time you visit our amphitheater, you will all bow down to me as your king—and the games will be rather more exciting. Please file out in an orderly manner, and return your togas to the costume department on the way out."

I thought this speech confirmed what Billy had told me. Bunyip was getting ready to be installed as king of everything—Kkhkktonos was about to make his comeback.

When the bus brought us back to Brown-Sparrow, I went to find Melvin.

"Billy the Phantom Bellboy says that tonight is the twelve thousandth full moon since the last time Kkhkktonos tried to resurge," I said.

"Wow, that's some news," Melvin said.

"It's going to happen at that coliseum they built," I said.

"Makes sense," Melvin said. "Probably they'll have a little ceremony before they go out and start unleashing chaos, kicking over buses, biting people in half, and all that."

"So, I figure I'd better go there and . . . what is it exactly I'm supposed to do?"

"Put a stop to it, obviously," Melvin said. "We can't have enormous carnivores running all over town."

"What do I do, just tell them to cut it out?"

"You could try that," Melvin said.

"Are you coming with me?"

"I'd like to, of course," Melvin said. "But I have to go with Crazy Wig. Besides, this is something you have to do alone."

"You're wearing a bowling shirt. Why are you wearing a bowling shirt? And that's a bowling ball bag, isn't it? Are you going bowling? Civilization may be ending tonight, and you're going bowling?"

"We're up against another team of shamans from West Covina. It will be the match of the year. I wish you could come."

"But . . . what about me?"

"Of course, we're terribly proud of you, being a shaman and so young and all."

"I'm not a shaman!"

"You keep saying that. You'll be fine. You can handle this."

"What makes you so sure? How do you know I can handle it?"

"Because you are the guy with the turtle."

CHAPTER 77

Twelve Thousandth Full Moon

The moon was just rising as I entered the coliseum. Slipping into the studio grounds had been easy. There didn't appear to be anyone around. I made my way up the ramps, and through the corridors, and then into the amphitheater.

There were big lights illuminating the arena. It had been flooded, filled with water, and was the size of a small lake. In the reflected light, I could see that the stands were full, but not with people in togas. The whole place was filled with gigantic predators: cave lions, huge bears, saber-tooth cats, and lots and lots of dire wolves. They were standing, some of them with their bodies spanning two or three rows of seats, and all of them perfectly still. They looked like statues, but they were real. I could see them breathing, and I could smell them. Several thousand dire wolves put out an unforgettable aroma. All of them were gazing into the arena, their eyes glowing.

The animals seemed to be in some kind of trance—they paid no attention to me, and I was able to move among them. It was amazing how big some of them were, especially close up. I made my way down to the parapet at the edge of the arena.

Sholmos Bunyip, wearing a gold Roman breast-plate and a gold helmet, was standing on the *suggestum,* chanting and mumbling. Most of what he was saying was gibberish and nonsense syllables, but now and then there was a phrase I could understand.

"Humma hummma . . . goo goo . . . manifest destiny . . . waka waka . . . power to the proletariat . . . ish kabibble . . . new world order . . . remember the Maine . . . hoo hoo . . . thousand points of light . . . we don't want to fight, but by jingo . . . oop shoop . . . guns or butter . . . lebensraum . . . no child left behind . . . city on a hill . . . I feel your pain . . . walla walla bing bang . . . day that will live in infamy . . . who put the overalls in Mrs. Murphy's chowder."

He was clean out of his mind, glassy-eyed, and a little scarier than the thousands of prehistoric carnivores listening to his weird speech. I knew what he was doing. He was the warm-up guy. He was getting the crowd ready for the appearance of Kkhkktonos. The animals were not in a trance—they were rapt, they were focused. Every glowing red eye was fixed on a spot in the middle of the fake lake, every breath was restrained, every tiny carnivorous brain was waiting, anticipating.

It felt a little lonely, being the only rational creature, and also the most likely snack, in the midst of all those meat-eaters. I really couldn't see any way that I was going to leave that place uneaten and in one piece. To my own surprise, the idea didn't bother me as much as I would have thought. *If I am going to be eaten, then eaten I will be,* I thought. But first I had to do my turtle-hero thing . . . and I still didn't know what it was!

The moon rose over the top of the coliseum. Little waves appeared on the surface of the water. Then it began to bubble and boil. Wisps of vapor rose. Bunyip was babbling faster and louder. The animals were breathing heavier.

The water began to swirl. There was a dark vortex right in the middle of it. It got darker.

"Kkhkktonos! Kkhkktonos! Kkhkktonos!" Bunyip was saying. The animals were breathing noisily.

Then a waterspout. It got higher and higher. Something dark was emerging.

"KKHKKTONOS! KKHKKTONOS! KKHKK-TONOS!"

Snort. Roar. Rumble. Pant.

"KKHKKTONOS!"

He was rising up. Very big. Black. More black than black. Darker than the darkest darkness. A black hole in the blackest black there ever was. Pulsating, shimmering, sucking at my eyes. And big! So big! And so bad! This was Kkhkktonos, no doubt about it, and he was no one to mess with.

Bunyip was shrieking, the animals were shrieking, Kkhkktonos was shining, if you can imagine something shining with darkness. He was towering up, higher than the top of the amphitheater. He radiated power—you could feel it. Definitely no one to mess with. The animals were stirring, roaring, and bellowing. The wolf stink was overpowering. Bunyip had fainted.

And then I, Neddie Wentworthstein, having no idea what I was doing, or why, messed with him. I jumped up on the parapet, holding my turtle in my fist, and shouted, "I am the guy! I am the guy with the turtle!"

CHAPTER 78

I Am the Guy

Everything went quiet. Dead quiet. I heard a few droplets of water splash to the surface of the flooded arena. Then, silence. Kkhkktonos towered over everything. None of the animals was breathing. Time was standing still. Then, I heard someone singing, softly. I knew the song—it was the one I had sung with the great turtle. I wondered where it was coming from, and who could be singing it. It was me! I sang louder. My voice filled the huge amphitheater. I felt powerful. I didn't know what I was doing or why, but I felt that if I kept singing I could make Kkhkktonos shrivel, vanish, sink out of sight.

And then Kkhkktonos spoke. He spoke in a voice

and in a language not heard on earth in thousands of years. It was pain to hear it, way deep in my ears. It was a black voice, thick and sticky and burning like hot lava. Ugly, creepy, filthy voice. And even though it sounded like air escaping from a huge balloon, I understood what he said.

"Somebody, eat that kid."

Several thousand dire wolves lunged, and at the same moment, I launched myself, still singing, into the air, and executed a very good dive, right into the water—where Kkhkktonos was!

The wolves swarmed into the water after me. They were good swimmers, the wolves, and they caught up with me right away. They paddled madly through the water, open-mouthed, their enormous teeth flashing. And some of them were on me in seconds, snapping and biting.

But they were hardly able to put a scratch on my carapace. Their fangs glanced off the scutes that made up the outer layer of my shell. Underneath the shell was strong bone, rigid and heavy, connected with my spinal column and ribs. Beneath, I was protected by my plastron, tough and thick and smooth—nothing for a wolf to bite into. I could have tucked my scaly feet in between my upper and lower shells and pulled my head in if I needed to be more protected—but I didn't have to. I was already too big for the wolves to do the least harm.

I was getting bigger and bigger. I was enormous. I think I was as big as the whole fake Coliseum Sholmos Bunyip had built. The coliseum was gone, by the way. No sign of it. No sign of anything, actually— just water. Big water. Endless water. A whole world of water.

These things, this becoming a turtle and then a turtle of stupendous size, then bigger than stupendous, and the spreading of Bunyip's fake lake to an endless ocean, seemed to be taking place in a few seconds—or a million years. There was no way for me to tell the difference. And I was busy singing the ancient turtle song, and didn't really care.

What I cared about was the next thing I had to do. This was simple. All I had to do was hold still, floating just below the surface, while friendly creatures piled cool mud on my back. Lots of mud. Heavy mud. Mud with trees growing. Mud with mountains. Mud with rivers, birds, animals, humans.

I sang the turtle song while all this mud-bringing and mud-building was going on. I was happy to hold still for it. I was happy to be of help. As the mud-world got heavy, another turtle, as large as myself, rose up under me and helped support me on his back. Under him, another turtle came, and another, down into the darkness.

CHAPTER 79

Pop!

I really liked being the Great Turtle, and supporting all of North America, or the world, or creation, on my back. I'd have thought a job like that would get boring, but it didn't. I could have done it forever. I had almost forgotten all about being Neddie.

Until I popped out of a little pond at the La Brea Tar Pits. I, Neddie, the same one I'd been before I met Kkhkktonos in the coliseum. Except for being all wet, with creosote on me, I was the same as I'd been. Everything else looked to be the same as it had been too: the little wire fences around the ponds—I had to climb over one to get out—the traffic on Wilshire Boulevard, all just the same. I even had the stone turtle in my pocket—I'll keep it until it's time to give it to the next person.

I like it here. I've been coming here a lot. I sit on this bench, with my parakeet, Henry, on my shoulder. I've been writing down everything that happened to me in this big school notebook. And I've got it all written, pretty much right up to the moment. I was going to write about what happened to Bunyip, and Seamus, and Aaron Finn, and Iggy and Billy the Phantom Bellboy, and what they are doing . . . but I've run out of space. It seems I have come to the last line of the last page.

The adventures continue in another
weird and wonderful tale
by Daniel Pinkwater!

CHAPTER 1

Room Full of Spooks

When I got home from school, my room was full of ghosts . . . again! They were being invisible, but I could feel the cold spots in the air.

"Did I speak to you ectoplasms about this, or did I not?" I asked the empty room.

Silence. The ghosts were dummying up.

"Rudolph Valentino! I can smell your lousy cigar!"

There was a faint smell of cigar smoke, the trademark of the ghostly Valentino, so I knew he was among them. And my bedspread was rumpled. Probably they were sitting on my bed, playing cards.

"Look, you spectres—this is a young girl's bedroom,

not a club! Why do you have to hang out here all the time? You have an eight-story hotel to haunt. There's a complete apartment reserved for your personal use. Why don't you stay there? It's the nicest one in the whole building." The management had sealed off a large apartment because it was way too haunted for living guests to put up with. The hope was that if they gave the ghosts their own space they wouldn't haunt the rest of the hotel so much. Some hope.

"We get bored," Rudolph Valentino said. "It's nothing but ghosts there."

"So you crowd in here so you can bore me, and stink up my room," I said. I was mad. I really liked most of the ghosts, but a woman is entitled to some privacy. Grumbling and mumbling, the ghosts climbed out my bedroom window, made their way along the ledge, and climbed into the window of the apartment that had belonged to Valentino in 1927. I had been in the apartment lots of times. Like the ghosts, I had to climb out my window and go along the narrow ledge to get in, which was a little scary to do if you weren't already dead.

The Hermione is not a regular hotel in the sense that people check in for a couple of nights or a week. It's all apartments, some tiny and some quite large. People live in it for months at a stretch, or all the time. It was quite the fancy address when my father first came to Hollywood in the days of the silent movies.

You can see what a deluxe sort of place it was. It has

architecture all over it. There are rough plaster walls, old-fashioned light fixtures made of hammered iron, fancy tile floors, and dark, heavy woodwork with carvings and decorations on it. There are tapestries that hang from iron things that look like spears, and a couple of suits of armor standing around. It looks like a movie set. It's a combination of old Spanish California and the Middle Ages, with some *Arabian Nights* thrown in.

I have lived in the Hermione all my life. I know the old hotel from top to bottom. I have been in all of the apartments, the basement, the laundry, and the restaurant that's been closed for years, and I know about the deserted tennis courts and the second, unused, and hidden swimming pool where the enormous turtle lives. I know things about the hotel that Mr. Glanvill, the manager, does not know. Chase, my favorite ghost, was the one who showed me where to find the master key someone had mislaid a long time ago. It opens every door in the place except the one to Valentino's apartment where all the ghosts hang out, because the door lock is rusted solid.

Chase is not the ghost of a person. She is the ghost of a black bunny rabbit. She has been sort of my own personal ghost since I was a baby. We are able to talk, which is something you can't do with a living bunny. Chase changes size. Usually, she is bunny-size, but I have seen her get to be as large as a German shepherd dog.

Rudolph Valentino is the ghost most people would know about, because he was a big movie star in the 1920s—but the oldest ghost, and the one who should be most famous, really, is La Brea Woman. Valentino doesn't compare to La Brea Woman for being distinguished. She is the only human whose bones have been pulled out of the La Brea Tar Pits. She lived about nine thousand years ago. She is the oldest human ever found in Southern California. Plus, she was murdered—someone knocked her on the head with a rock. We are all proud of La Brea Woman. And she's a nice ghost. She's shorter than I am, in her early twenties, and she always has her hair in curlers and wears sunglasses with pink frames and fuzzy pink slippers. She is friendly and cheerful, and talks a blue streak in some ancient dialect that hasn't been heard on earth in thousands of years.

I don't know exactly how many ghosts live in the Hermione—at least a dozen, maybe more. Not all of them like to communicate—they just haunt, appear and disappear, walk the corridors—some of them moan, or cry, or make ghostly laughter. Chase is the only ghost with whom I can have a conversation. Valentino will exchange a few words with me—but that's just his polite nature. Also, he may be nice to me because he knew my father in the old days.